Green Bike
a group novel

by
Kevin Rabas,
Mike Graves
and Tracy Million Simmons

A MEADOWLARK BOOK

Meadowlark (an imprint of Chasing Tigers Press)
Copyright © 2014 Kevin Rabas, Mike Graves, Tracy Million Simmons
meadowlark-books.com

Cover by Eric Sonnakolb, ericsonnakolb.com

This book was written collaboratively as part of the Emporia independent meeting group collective of the Kansas Authors Club (KAC). Views expressed are the authors' own and are not representative of KAC.

ISBN-13: 978-0692266168 (Meadowlark)
ISBN-10: 069226616X

Green Bike

a group novel

by
Kevin Rabas,
Mike Graves
and Tracy Million Simmons

For the Emporia Writers Group
Members Past, Present & Future

McGuffin (məˈɡʌfɪn) —n
an object or event in a book or a film that serves as the impetus for
the plot

That Damned Green Bike
Kevin Rabas

Calvin was suspicious when Bea came home to her apartment with a bike, a classic green Schwinn, the kind Harley always rode around town. Harley ran the bike shop, and Calvin knew Bea didn't have the dough for a new bike. She said it was a gift or a loan, she wasn't sure, but Harley told her to take it. Calvin had always wondered about Harley's intentions, and now he had some evidence. There was something there.

Harley wore retro clothes, often a mechanic's jumper with someone else's name on the lapel, "Dave," or "Joshua," or "Stan." Harley brought Bea chamomile tea when she visited the bike shop, brewed the tea in a round metal steeper and put a few flower petals from his jasmine plant on top; they floated in the yellow, soporific water. He winked at Bea when she passed the bike shop, "Jake's Bikes." Calvin didn't even know if there was a Jake, but Harley ran the shop, kept up the name, and hit on Bea every chance he got.

Calvin loved Bea and didn't want to appear jealous. He brought home a bread loaf-sized Saraswati to her. She was seated with her sitar guitar on an enormous blooming lotus, its petals surrounding her like a feather boa. That same day the green bike showed up. Bea looked at the Saraswati and kissed Calvin, then claimed she had "things to do" and rode her bike into town. Calvin lit incense, watched the Saraswati in the yellow embers of autumn, Manhattan-Kansas light. A shadow fell on the figure's forehead.

That night, Bea didn't come home. Calvin wrapped Saraswati in one of Bea's hand towels, put it in his backpack, and walked home to his room, part of a big yellow house with chipping paint divided into five units. He rarely slept there anymore. Bea's was where he had slept the past semester. He spent evenings and mornings at Bea's side while they graded freshman composition papers. To these English GTAs and masters candidates, this was what candlelight romance looked like: dim light, red pens, quiet ruminations over grammar and substance, written argument and rhetoric, over Tohlman's warrant and claim, over thesis, body, and conclusion. And so it ended that morning when Bea didn't come home, and the green bike was gone. Calvin cried in his apartment. He set the statuette on the highest shelf, and it seemed to watch him as he packed Bea's things into a laundry basket. Black lace bras and panties were the last things he packed. He thought he'd kept nothing, but weeks later, he found a bottle of nail polish remover under the bathroom sink. Bea had always painted and repainted her nails.

Stolen Bike

Mike Graves

Miles stepped out the back door of the English building, moved away the obligatory thirty feet and lit a cigarette. When he'd taken a drag, his cell phone rang.

"I have an hour," the voice said. "Can you make it?"

Miles dropped his cigarette and looked at his watch. Twelve blocks there, twelve blocks back, a class in just over an hour. Damn. It would be cutting it close, but hormones swamped reason.

"Yeah, I'll be there."

He rang off, cursing his decision to walk to campus today instead of driving his rusty Cavalier. He'd have to jog. He reached the corner of the building and noticed the bike rack. Three bikes were chained to the rack, but a fourth one, an old green Schwinn with balloon tires and a bell on the handlebars was leaning against the rack unchained. Miles looked around. Students were drifting along the sidewalk, chatting on cell phones or plugged into iPods. Miles snatched the bike and pedaled south under the arch and off the campus. It took six minutes to reach her door. She opened it before he knocked.

"That was fast," she said with a smile.

"Yeah, well I had incentive. Where's Jimmy?"

"Out with one of his dopey friends gathering guns and ammo and deer piss and whatever else they use to kill and maim defenseless creatures. He said he'd be back for lunch."

"Terrific, Wanda. If we get caught, he'll not only be angry, he'll be armed."

Wanda moved closer to him and whispered, "Hush," into his ear. She tilted her head back, and he kissed her and led her backward toward the bedroom.

Wanda had been a student of his, of course, and he knew he was being stupid. He really had listened to his senior colleagues who had warned him against this sort of thing.

"Stay away from the coeds, Miles," they said. "They're trouble. Your brain is larger than your penis. Use it."

And he'd listened. He wanted tenure, dammit. He didn't need this. Still, he'd succumbed, and his life had become a cliché. She'd taken his Milton class, and he should have realized something was up when she showed more interest in Milton's divorce tracts than *Paradise Lost*. She'd even written her final paper on the tracts, analyzing Milton's unhappy first marriage and the relationships that followed. Miles had read the rough drafts, made appropriate comments and suggestions to improve the paper, and had listened as Wanda told him the problems in her own marriage. He moved from teacher, to counselor, to lover in the space of sixteen weeks.

They were nodding off when the cat jumped onto the bed. Miles looked at his watch. Eleven minutes till class started. He dressed quickly, gave Wanda a hug and took the stairs two at a time. He jumped on the green bike, and as he rounded the corner, he saw Jimmy's pickup coming toward him. He lowered his head, but noticed a guy sitting next to Jimmy looking at him. Miles didn't recognize the face, but the guy was wearing a ball cap that said "Jake's Bikes" across the front. Six minutes later Miles parked the bike in the rack and dashed into the English building.

Clothes Left in Washer
Kevin Rabas

Calvin remembered that he had a load of his own laundry in Bea's apartment complex quarter washer, a machine run by inserting 75 cents, three coins at once. He didn't mind about the underwear and the socks. He didn't mind about the t-shirts. But there were a few indispensable items in that load, dress shirts, go-out shirts, shirts he needed to teach and to go out on the town and look for another love, if Bea never came back, and in this moment he realized: she might not. He loved her, and he'd wait for her, but he was not going to wait at home. He was going to go for a drink. In Aggieville, it was Halloween.

He called up Bea's rival and asked her for a date. She'd said, "Find me in Aggieville. If you can find me, we'll go out. We'll go out on the town together." When he asked about her costume, she replied, "You think I'll tell you that? It'd be too easy for a man like you. Use your powers of perception. In a few short months, you'll be a Master of the Universe."

That was the title creative writing professors gave to new creative writing MAs. With few to no jobs out there and the available ones going to the top notch writers and teachers, the title was an academic joke. Calvin tried not to think about it and wrote to block his fears. Every night, he wrote. He wrote in the morning. He wrote in between classes, and he tried like hell to teach. Usually, he performed well. But there were the insanely stressful days. On days like that, he'd held Bea's hand on the way to class. It meant he was tied to something, to someone, and Bea was beautiful. In horn-rimmed glasses and thrift-store clothes, she was bookishly beautiful. And she chose those clothes wisely, like a *fashionista*. Many women could see that, and squinted their eyes in envy after Bea strolled by.

Calvin decided he could pull off masquerading as Jacques Cousteau. With the hood pulled up, he could go incognito, should he see Bea among them, Bea with her green bike parked out front.

Julie didn't see Calvin when he walked into Annie Mae's. Although he wore a longshoreman's cap and a yellow raincoat, she most likely didn't see him because she sat near the back. She wore a devil costume, complete with a red forked tail and a pitchfork. Calvin wasn't looking for a devil or a demon lover, but he looked closely around the bar, and walked right by Julie. She didn't say anything.

Mailroom Banter

Kevin Rabas

Bea had held a crush for Miles for months. In the department mailroom, in a moment of boredom and bravado, Bea declared her eccentric wish. The GTAs filed in and pulled the pink and blue and white slips of paper from their little office boxes, those open wooden squares like the kind kindergartners keep their shoes in. Bea said, "I'd like to press him up against the lectern and kiss him, see what that would do. I bet he'd kiss back."

Slim Sally looked like a younger version of Shelley Duvall, who portrayed Olive Oyl in the Popeye film. She quipped, "Bea, you can say it, but you'd never do it. You just don't have the balls."

Bea hated Slim Sally and retorted, "Just you watch. Someday I may just do it. Just you watch."

"I'll be there," Sally said. "Bring it. I'm all eyes. I'm ready. To. Watch."

Bea tapped Slim Sally on the nose with one finger. "I'll bet you want to watch," and smirked and winked and walked off.

Miles, Moll, and Milton
Mike Graves

"So what is Defoe telling us about Moll Flanders? Is she a common criminal, a prostitute, a victim of her time, or maybe all three?"

Miles stared at the vapid expressions on their faces. The class was titled "Rogues and Outcasts, a Seminar on Picaresque Literature," and Miles always looked forward to teaching it. He'd been intrigued by the genre since his grad school days, and it was a pleasant respite from the dour Milton. This was an advanced class, open to seniors and graduate students who were generally studious, and Miles enjoyed the banter and the intellectual give and take. Today, however, the chemistry wasn't working. Everyone, himself included, seemed to be suffering from the doldrums.

"Come on, anyone? What are your thoughts on Moll?"

"She was a prostitute."

"That's it? She was a prostitute? Does that sum up Moll's life?"

"Well, she slept with a lot of men for money."

"True, but remember this was 17th-century England. A woman didn't have many choices then."

"I don't care when or where it was. She shouldn't have prostituted herself. I could never do anything like that."

This from a twenty-something coed wearing Prada sneakers that probably set her old man back about $400. And so it went. Another generation of students with precious little experience and all of the answers. Miles glanced at his watch. Thirty more minutes. He allowed himself a moment to reflect on his latest academic achievement. A paper he had written, "Muse, Mystery, and Mythology in Milton's Nativity Ode," had been accepted by *Milton Quarterly*, and for the moment he was the darling of the department. He had been working hard, and it felt good. It had been over two weeks since he'd last seen Wanda, and the break had been more welcome than he would have expected. They had agreed it was too risky for him to call her, even on her cell phone, and she hadn't called him. At first he wondered why, but after a few days he quit dwelling on it. He loved being with Wanda, but he hated complications, and seeing her was a major complication. On the one hand he loved Wanda, but on the other hand he loved simplicity, and life with Wanda was not simple. Miss Prada sneakers raised her hand, and Miles nodded toward her.

"Moll Flanders married her brother. That's disgusting."

"Actually, she married her half-brother. She didn't know it at the time, and as soon as she found out she dissolved the marriage."

"Well, it's still disgusting."

It must be nice living in a world of absolutes, Miles thought. He had once lived in that world. Black and white. Yes and no. Right and wrong. Now everything seemed to have so many shades of gray.

"Instead of focusing on Moll's morals, why don't we consider her situation and discuss her options. She became a thief to survive. She stole what she needed to live. Isn't that justified?"

The class was divided. Most thought stealing was acceptable in life or death situations, but others argued that stealing might jeopardize the lives of the victims and should never be condoned. A young lady in the back of the room who had not spoken during the class added her voice. Miles recognized her as one of the graduate teaching assistants. She was bookishly beautiful, in horn-rimmed glasses and thrift store clothes.

"Moll Flanders should have stolen a bicycle. She could have used it to visit her lovers."

The class groaned.

"That's stupid. They didn't even have bicycles back then."

But the young woman held her ground and ignored the comments around her. She stared at Miles. Miles stared back. Finally he spoke. Or maybe he whispered.

"Class dismissed."

***

"You are so busted, dude."

Bea stood in front of his desk with a smirk on her face. She had come into his office and closed the door. Miles had immediately gotten up and opened it again. Now he sat behind his desk. He had not asked Bea to sit down. He held his head in his hands and looked down as he spoke.

"Make that Professor Dude, Bea."

"Yeah, whatever. You are still busted. I know you took my bike. The guy who gave it to me saw you riding it."

"Is this guy your boyfriend?"

"That's none of your business. Why did you take it? Were you using it to visit a lover?"

Miles shook his head and groaned. He looked up, but not at Bea. His eyes fell on the coatrack in the corner of his office. His academic robe and cape were hanging on the rack along with his dark blue hood. He noticed a thread dangling from the hem of the robe. It was coming unraveled. He'd have to get it fixed.

"I was in a hurry. I had to run an errand. I didn't have much time, and I didn't think the owner would mind."

"Yeah, right. What kind of errand were you running in that neighborhood?"

"To use your phrasing, that's none of your business."

Bea was still smiling.

"Hey, chill out Professor Dude. You can use the bike anytime. It'll be our secret."

She leaned forward and whispered.

"Maybe before this is over, we'll be sharing more secrets."

She stood up, blew him a kiss, and left the office. Miles sat without moving for a moment before reaching for his cell phone. He knew he wasn't supposed to call Wanda, but he needed to talk to her. He hit speed dial, and the phone rang once before he heard a voice.

"The number you have called cannot be completed as dialed…"

Miles stared at the phone. He tried again. This time he passed over speed dial and punched in each number.

"The number you have called cannot be completed as dialed…"

My god, he thought. What next? Miles crossed the room and looked out the window. Students were walking on the sidewalk, shuffling through fallen leaves. A few cars were winding down the drive. And a young woman in thrift store clothes pedaled a green bike across the campus.

Door Poem
Kevin Rabas

Calvin didn't find Julie anywhere, and as Halloween turned into November, as darkness started turning into early morning light, he stopped by the house Julie lived in with three other girls. He knew where it was. Julie wasn't there. It was five a.m. There were two young women passed out on an old, golden couch, the TV on, playing *Episode IV: The Empire Strikes Back*. It was at the beginning, the men shooting and getting stomped on by Imperial Walkers in the snow, in the cold of Hoth. Calvin sat down on the couch, and one of the women woke up. She had a small length from a bike chain around her neck and a padlock holding it, like a choker, above her Adam's apple.

"Who are you?" she said.

"Calvin. I had a date with Julie in Aggieville, but I didn't find her. So, I came here."

"Oh, you're that Calvin. I think she likes you. She said, 'He needs to dress better, though.'"

Calvin pulled a small notebook from his front pocket and started writing, quickly.

"Which one's her door?"

"That one," chain lady said.

"I'll leave her a note."

"Make it love poetry," chain lady said. "She likes poetry."

"Does she?" Calvin said. "I'm drunk. But I think I can write a few couplets or string together some haiku."

"Do it," said chain lady. "You can do it, sport. What are you anyway?"

"Jacques Cousteau," Calvin said. "Couldn't you tell?"

"Shit, you look like a weatherman or a longshoreman or some little snotty kid expecting rain on a sunny day."

"Thanks," Calvin said.

"Any time. Dress better. She'll like you."

Chain lady closed her eyes. Calvin left his message, slipped it under the door, and left. As he left, morning dawning, a green bike zipped by a few blocks away. That wasn't Bea on it.

Miles to Go...
Mike Graves

Miles left the Halloween party swimming in a sea of eighty-proof courage. He wasn't quite hammered, but he did feel like bullets would bounce off his chest. He hadn't felt like partying, but the department chair had arranged the faculty mixer, and he'd been obliged to attend.

"Come as a favorite literary character," she'd said to everyone. "Won't that be fun?"

Miles had selected Quasimodo, and now here he was, semi-drunk, bent over, and shuffling through Aggieville looking like a freak. He thought about stopping at a bar for a drink, but the loud music and raucous laughter didn't suit his mood. He'd go on home. He walked another block and spotted something familiar. He wasn't sure, but as he got closer he grew more certain. Yes, that was it, leaning against a brick wall, still without a chain. The green bike.

Miles, or rather Quasimodo, glanced around. Several students were in costume, he-ing and she-ing, drinks in hand, and no one was paying attention to him. He jumped on the bike, hunched over the handlebars, and pedaled away.

Hell, she said I could borrow it anytime, he thought. It was after midnight, and the little ones had finished trick-or-treating and gone to bed. A few teenage pranksters still roamed the streets, but most of the homes were dark. Miles felt alive as he sailed through the black night. A couple of teenagers spotted him and jumped into the road in front of him. Miles didn't slow down.

"Sanctuary!" he yelled as he pedaled toward his Esmeralda. "Sanctuary!"

The teens jumped back and stared at the hump-backed fool on the bike.

"Sanctuary!"

Miles had no plan. He barely had a thought. He just knew he had to find Wanda.

"Sanctuary!"

He jumped off the bike, ran through the yard, and pounded on the door. The house was dark. He pounded again, and a light came on. The door cracked open, and a pair of eyes stared at him. Quasimodo stared back. The door opened a bit more. The eyes belonged to an elderly man. The man spoke.

"What do you want?"

Miles was stunned. He must have the wrong house. He stepped back and looked at the number next to the door. This was her house. The man spoke again.

"I said, what do you want?"

Miles tottered a bit.

"Trick or treat?"

"Trick or treat? You're drunk!"

The door started to close.

"Wait! Are Jimmy and Wanda here?"

"No, they're gone. Now go home and go to bed."

And the door slammed shut. Quasimodo stumbled off the porch, climbed on the green bike and pedaled into the night.

Brady's Last Summer

Tracy Million Simmons

This wasn't the way he was supposed to spend his last summer before heading off to college, his last summer of childhood, though most of his friends would be offended if he referred to them as children. He would have been offended himself, except that's the way he'd begun to think of it. His summer—perhaps the final, carefree summer of his life—had been stolen from him.

Brady let the soup reach a boil and then carefully ladled it into the bowl. He grabbed one ice cube from the freezer and dropped it in, stirring. He knew from experience that one cube would cool it just enough for her. She couldn't take things hot these days, nor could she take them excessively cold. He set the soup and the spoon on the tray with extra napkins. She always needed the extra napkins. It made his heart sick, but she had developed a tendency to drool... or sometimes just to spit whatever he was feeding her back at him. He poured half a can of Ensure into a juice glass. This way he would know if she was actually drinking it and not just tilting the can to her lips in pretend. He picked up the tray and looked at it for a moment. He put it back down on the counter and dashed outside.

His mother's flower gardens in the front of the house were a wreck. It was obvious that nobody was taking care of them. But it was Brady's job to keep the lawn mowed so that the neighbors didn't complain, keep after the house, and to take care of his mother, of course. He'd tried to make himself weed the flower beds several times, but he always found excuses. He was too tired. He'd rather clean inside the house. Something about the monotony of pulling weeds gave his mind time to wander and it tended to wander to places he couldn't afford to go right now. Taking care of his mother was the least he could do, and he was trying like hell not to resent his obligation.

He grabbed a handful of flowers—they were actually quite bountiful in this season of neglect—and took a moment to separate the weeds from the collection. Back in the kitchen, he took a vase from the shelf and filled it with water. He placed the flowers in the vase on the tray. That was better. Maybe it would bring a smile to his mother's face.

When he entered her room, her head was tilted toward the window. He and his father had rearranged the bedroom furniture before his dad had left for work this time. Brady thought she might enjoy a view of the neighborhood. He was disappointed to see that her eyes were shut, but when he sat the tray down on the table by her bed, she said, "There's someone new across the street."

He'd noticed. The moving truck, anyway. New families with potential kids as new friends didn't thrill him the way they did when he was a kid.

"You should introduce yourself," she said. Her eyes were still closed. "There's a girl about your age. She's pretty. Red hair."

This he had not noticed. He found himself looking through his mother's window across the street into an empty yard. He didn't even see that she had opened her eyes until she said, "You brought flowers. They are beautiful."

Brady felt himself relaxing. His mother was being talkative and that was a good sign. It meant she would likely sit up and spoon her soup into her own mouth. It meant she would quiz him on his housekeeping techniques and advise him on things he might be overlooking, like the grease buildup on the hood from the gas stove and that it was time to change the filter so the air conditioner would continue to run properly.

He watched her lift the juice glass and drink greedily. If he'd had any idea, he would have brought the rest of the can to take advantage of the moment. She returned the glass to the tray and leaned forward. He arranged her pillows so that she sat up a little straighter, doing his best not to touch her bony back and be reminded of just how thin his mother had become. It was hard enough to look at her face, eyes too small in sunken orbits, or to watch her thin lips spread over teeth that seemed too large for her pained smile. Everything about her looked mismatched these days.

"I can get you more." He motioned to the near-empty juice glass.

"No, this is fine," his mother said.

He arranged the tray with its sturdy legs across her lap and relaxed as she began to eat the soup. He let his eyes wander to the yard across the street. His friends had actually been very supportive and accommodating, at least at first. The first week after graduation they'd come to his house to spend the evening watching movies and hanging out. He wasn't much of a host, however, and he could tell it made them uncomfortable, just knowing she was up there. He'd had to check on her several times. He had helped her to the bathroom. He wouldn't blame them for not wanting to be around. When his dad returned, five weeks in Guatemala this time, his friends would throw a good party and he would go out and make up for some of his lost partying time.

"You know what I've been thinking about?" Her voice startled him. It was strong and clear. She sounded almost like her old self, his mother before the cancer had come. "I've been thinking about my bicycle. It looks like lovely bicycling weather."

He'd noticed his mother's classic green Schwinn in the garage just the day before. Its tires were both flat. It was covered in dust and cobwebs. The sight of it had made him choke up a little. His mother had ridden that bike everywhere before she'd gotten sick.

"You know what, Mom? I'm going to give that old bike a tune-up," he said. "I think it could use a little TLC. I'll fix the tires. Oil the chain. It'll be all ready for you, as soon as you are well enough to ride."

She looked at him and smiled. They both knew she wouldn't be riding anywhere again.

Halloween, Calvin Finds Julie
Kevin Rabas

"Before going out," Julie said, "my friend Sandra—you call her Chain Lady—cooked some steaks on our little round charcoal grill.

We sat the grill a little ways into the street, so it was away from the house, and we cooked and drank, cooked and drank, until we forgot about the grill, and burned those cheap steaks. So we took the steaks and loaded them into Sandra's car, and we sped through Aggieville and through the side streets near it, lobbing steaks out onto the sidewalk and onto the patches of grass. Hey. Free steaks."

Calvin looked at Julie. This seemed to him to be a story of decadence, but he didn't say anything. He looked into Julie's eyes, which were green, like the shallows along Tuttle Creek Lake, the lake with the Corps of Engineers bridge stretching across it, the lake where the students went to kiss and drink and watch the moon.

Julie put her small hand on Calvin's chest, and said, "Aren't you glad you finally found me?" Calvin found Julie walking home. He'd walked all around Aggieville looking for her, and then, when he had given up and started walking back home, there she was, in red, like a devil, with three fallen angels with bent burnt black wings following her. They had all gone home to freshen up, drink cheaply a few last swigs before going out again. Calvin was tired. He couldn't believe they weren't.

"Yes," Calvin said. "What now?"

"I loved your letter. Write me another one."

"What about tonight?"

"You look tired, sweetie. Go home. Come back when you've written me that letter. Call first. You know where to find me."

The wind picked up, and a gust blew in through Aggieville, through the red brick buildings and up the sidewalks, lifting newspapers and sales receipts as it swept, full of force and lift even on into the side streets. When the wind passed Calvin and the girls, their wings fluttered, and Calvin thought they just might take off and swift into the night, into the clouds, their shadows passing the moon. I must be drunk, Calvin thought, and went home.

...Before I Sleep
Mike Graves

Quasimodo pedaled through Aggieville. It was very late. Most revelers had gone home. The bars had closed. A few stragglers lingered on the walks, chatting together. Miles noticed a dog, then another and another on the walks and in the streets. They seemed to be eating something and snapping and growling at each other. It was meat he supposed. It almost looked like they were eating steaks, but that made no sense. *Big deal. Nothing made sense anymore.*

He passed a young woman in a red devil costume surrounded by several others dressed as fallen angels. The devil woman was smiling at a young man. Quasimodo whispered "Sanctuary" to himself as he pedaled by.

Miles didn't stop in Aggieville. He was sure Bea was no longer around so he rode onto the campus and parked the bike in the rack outside the English building. She'd find it there later, if it still belonged to her. Maybe it didn't. Miles was unsure of this, unsure of everything it seemed. As he sobered he struggled to think clearly.

Later, lying in bed, Miles gazed at the ceiling. Wanda was gone. *Where? Why? Was she safe? Was she happy? Who was the old man living in her house?* And now a teaching assistant was coming on to Miles. *What did Bea see in him?*

Miles tried to think logically. He had a logical mind and tried to use it, even as he embraced life's absurdities. He'd started his undergraduate work at the University of Michigan, bent on becoming an engineer. Chemistry and calculus lessons had been daunting, and he struggled to maintain even average grades. In his drafting classes, he came to the realization that he couldn't look at a three-dimensional object and imagine the hidden lines, angles, and faces behind it. At the end of his first semester his only decent grades were in philosophy and English, both electives. He changed his major to English the next semester.

As Miles lay in bed, he thought about the choices he'd made, and like a true existentialist, accepted those choices as his. He didn't wonder how his life would have been different as an engineer. *People are alive today, because I never built a bridge*, he reasoned.

Now he was faced with new choices. He could let go of Wanda, accept her disappearance, and move on. He could let Bea come into his life. Would that last for an hour, a few days, or longer? Or he could go back to what he was before all this started: a simple, single, celibate, serious scholar. Miles mulled over this alliterative thought as his eyes drooped shut. As he drifted into sleep, his final thoughts turned to red devils and fallen angels.

Calvin Writes Julie a Poem
Kevin Rabas

Calvin wrote these lines:

I got a drink at almost every bar in Aggieville, looking for you.

I saw a man call on a woman that last time. She was an angel. At least for
that night,

wearing white and a tin foil halo. He said, "I'd do anything for you,"

and she said, "You already have, and it's not enough," and he banged

his head on the sidewalk until it bled. "I can't get your love

out of my head. I'd do anything for you," he said.

She said, "You already have. Stupid love. It makes you bloody your
forehead

for nothing, for a vision, a touch, a sense of beauty and order.

Women know beauty, but don't admire it like men. Go home.

Find yourself someone else. I'm no angel." And he left, alone, drunk,

his face running blood. He knew love. She knew love. It runs,

like blood on the forehead, like blood on the sidewalk, like blood

through our arteries and veins, quick with impression and lust,

mixing memory with desire until it's that perfect cocktail,

that drink you ask for and can never put down.

Calvin wondered if Julie would spot the Eliot and Millay quotes. He knew they said it better than he could. Oh well. If she figured it out, he'd know she was literate, literary, literati. If she didn't, he'd call it sampling, like in rap. Use what you know. Use what you love. Use what other people know and love, and call it part of your song.

Love Letter, Take 2
Kevin Rabas

That first letter didn't seem enough about love, about Calvin's new love for Julie. It seemed more like a testament to insane, crazy love, when it ends. This was a start, a starter love. Calvin thought, I've got to write a "new love" love poem. He started with what he knew.

I had put some sake into the microwave for 30 seconds,

and you came with a girlfriend to my door. The sake

overflowed. I left it to answer the door, seeing you there

in white cashmere and a red mini skirt, headed

into Aggieville, casual, bold, full of beauty and light;

your eyes were like blueberries in a bowl,

full of color and depth, dotted with water, sweet.

I wanted to reach out and touch your cheek, kiss you

in front of the guys, crowded on the couch, drinking

Coors and Miller and Jack, while I heated up some sake,

something I had learned to love traveling, and here

you were, full of spice. You took a sip from the small

porcelain cup, and said you liked it, drank half, and said,

"You drink the rest." "Don't like it?" "No," you said.

"We'll share it. You drink the rest. Besides," you said.

"afraid of my lips?" And I drank, and I drank, and I drank that night,

and nothing was as sweet as that first sip.

That wouldn't do. It was too full of backstory, too full of sake and beer and the feeling of wine with no roses. Calvin decided he'd try again in the morning. It was too late to write. Too late to write a love poem, tonight.

Wanda Rings
Mike Graves

October gave way to November. Scarlet and gold ceded to gray and brown. The once crisp foliage sparkling overhead now lay in damp, dark clumps on the ground and gathered in gutters and corners. Fall was Miles's favorite season. He looked to it as a time for fresh beginnings. Poets and writers had long considered fall synonymous with impending death, the final days before the onset of cold, cold winter, but Miles disagreed. He was a teacher, and fall meant a new semester, new students, new classes, a clean grade book, and the hope that this semester would bring him the brightest and best students eager to explore adventures in literature. That hope usually carried him through September and October, but often faded in November when students began losing energy, skipping classes, and offering lame excuses for late homework. This semester was no different.

Miles didn't blame his students. He hadn't been the most inspirational teacher this semester. He'd been distracted, touched by love, and he blamed himself. Miles sat in his office, brushing up notes for his Rogues and Outcasts class.

Fred Holland, one of his colleagues, stuck his head in the door.

"Hey, Miles, you know what the three best things in life are?"

"Enlighten me, Fred."

"A drink before and a cigarette after."

Miles listened to Fred's laughter as he moved down the hall.

Miles returned to his notes, and the phone rang. He picked up on the second ring and said, "hello."

"Hello, Miles. How are you?"

He clenched the phone and closed his eyes.

"Wanda."

"I needed to call you, Miles."

"Where are you? What's going on? What happened to you?"

"Miles, please, let me speak. I don't have much time. Just listen, OK?"

Miles breathed in and out several times.

"OK."

"Miles, I'm fine. I've been away with Jimmy. We've been on a cruise. I won't give you all of the details, but the thing you should know is that Jimmy and I have fallen in love again. We've fallen in love, Miles."

Miles shook his head.

"What about us?"

"There is no 'us,' Miles. I don't think there ever was. We found something we both needed at the time, and now we have to move on. I felt I owed you this call, but it's over, Miles."

"Can I see you one last time? Can we talk about this face to face?"

"No, Miles. We cannot see each other. It's over. Please don't try to reach me."

Wanda may have said more. She may have said, "I'll always care for you, Miles" or "I'll always remember you" or "I wish you nothing but good things, Miles," but he didn't hear anything after "…don't try to reach me." He dropped the phone on his desk. It was over.

Miles stared at the phone and shook his head. After a moment, he gathered his notes and shuffled out of his office. Down the hall, a classroom of students waited for another inspiring episode of Rogues and Outcasts.

Calvin's Letter to Julie, Take 3

Kevin Rabas

Your small, strong hands took the block of brown-gray clay

and thumped it onto the desk; you picked it, dropped it

shaped it; you took the air out

of the mud and clay and made it ready

to spin and shape and rise.

I didn't know you, but I saw you, working,

when I came to take a weekend class on wheel thrown

pottery; the wheel spun like the earth and made the clay

rise—against gravity; like hope, it rose.

I didn't know you, who you were, what secrets you held.

I watched your hands work the clay. I looked down at my own

hands, like two dumb roots, and watched yours,

covered in clay: where did the clay stop and your hands begin—

in strength, in beauty, your hands like two doves

rising from a puddle, rising from the rain.

"Good enough," Calvin said. He got in his blue Chevy S-10 Blazer, and swiftly turned the key. It wasn't so long a ways to Julie's. He put the letter in through the metal slot on the door. He picked a rose from out front and broke the head from the stem and pushed the petals in through the slot after the letter. The petals fell, a soft rain, onto the floor behind the door.

A Little Dessert
Mike Graves

Miles sat on a bar stool and munched on a turkey sandwich. Part of him was listening to Fred, who sat at his elbow, while another part was weighing his situation and new-found resolve. Miles wasn't over losing Wanda. He knew that. Does anyone ever fully recover from a lost love? Still, he'd promised himself he'd stay strong. Who was it who had said when you can't go on, the only thing remaining is to go on? Miles would go on. He'd find solace and comfort, as he always had, in his work. When life receded and reached an ebb, Miles turned to literature, to scholarly research, to reading and writing to carry him through. He was fortunate to have his work. He chuckled to himself. Only his mother, it seemed, truly understood him. Whenever he had a burst of creativity and energy, when he read hundreds of pages a night, or produced reams of scholarly drafts, his friends and colleagues would marvel at his productivity. Only his mother would wonder, "What's troubling you, Miles?"

Fred was speaking.

"So, Miles old man, what are your plans for the holidays?"

Miles swallowed and wiped his mouth with a napkin.

"Nothing big, Fred. I haven't given Thanksgiving much thought actually. I'll probably visit the folks. How about you?"

"Well, I'd like to go to Las Vegas for a few days, but Sharon wants to visit her family in Minnesota. That's what we'll do, I suppose. If we don't go for Thanksgiving, we'll have to go at Christmas, and I'd rather be anywhere but Minnesota in December."

Miles nodded. They were having lunch in one of those Aggieville establishments that served as a deli-by-day and a saloon-by-night. The place was crowded, and Miles and Fred had started to leave, but Fred had spotted two open stools at the bar. Students and faculty, sitting and standing, milled elbow-to-elbow. Now, as they were finishing, it had quieted some. The swarm of locusts had moved on.

"I have to run. What time is your next class, Miles?"

"Not until two."

"I have a class in ten minutes. Take your time, okay? I'll see you back in the office."

Fred dropped a few bucks on the bar and hurried out the door. Miles watched him turn the corner and went back to his sandwich. Frankly, he was happy to be alone for a moment. Tunes from a local radio station mingled with the low hum of voices. A waitress leaned over the bar toward him.

"Will there be anything else?"

Miles shook his head, and she took his money and turned to the register.

"How about some dessert?"

Miles turned around toward the voice. Bea was standing there, smiling at him, looking elegant as ever in her thrift store clothes. Behind her was another young woman, someone Miles had seen before, but he couldn't recall her name. She reminded him of Olive Oyl. Miles stood.

"Hello, Bea."

Bea said nothing at first. She continued smiling, but her expression changed somewhat. Her smile seemed frozen, her arms stiff, and she was beating her tiny fists against her thighs. When she spoke, her words caught in her throat.

"Hello, back at ya, Professor Dude."

She suddenly stepped forward, threw her arms around his neck, and planted her lips on his. She kissed him. She kissed him and held him, and without realizing it, Miles kissed back. They stood in each other's arms a brief moment. Somewhere in the background came the sounds of "Woo, woo!" and "Way to go!" and finally, "Get a room."

Bea dropped her arms and stepped back. Miles didn't speak. Bea didn't speak. She stood and grinned. Olive Oyl stared with an open mouth. Both women turned and hurried out the door. Miles watched them get on bicycles and pedal around the corner. Even after they disappeared, he could still hear the clanging of the little bell on the green bike.

Brady Meets Mary

Tracy Million Simmons

Brady pushed the old green Schwinn out of the garage and into the driveway. He looked up at the house, assuring himself that his mother could see his work space. He intended to clean the bike and replace the tubes, maybe ride it up and down the street a few times to make sure he'd worked all of the kinks out. As he worked, however, it became clear that the bike was in worse shape than he thought. Spots of rust were beginning to show through the green paint. His mother had always been meticulous in the care of her bike. So the plan to clean the bicycle became more of an act of disassembling it.

It didn't help that the red haired girl—the one his mother had called pretty—came out into the yard across the street to play with a young boy. A little brother, Brady hoped. It was hard to tell these days. He knew more than enough girls his age who already had children.

He found himself watching them without obviously watching; listening without obviously listening. It slowed his work and several times he found himself taking apart pieces of the bike he really hadn't intended to take apart. The chain from the derailleur. Then part of the derailleur itself. He didn't worry about how he would get the bike back together. He simply enjoyed the process of taking it apart. Even more, he enjoyed watching the red haired girl. The little boy called her Ma-wee, which Brady had eventually determined to be Mary rather than baby-talk for mother. With that burden off his mind, the girl grew more and more beautiful as he watched her play with the little boy while he disassembled his mother's old green bicycle.

Twice Brady went into the house, prompted by the alarm on his cell phone, to check on his mother. She was sleeping deeply both times, so he let her be. On his third trip into the house to check on her, she'd asked about his work on the bike.

"Looks like you are doing a very thorough job," she said, and then, "Have you met her yet?"

As sick as she was, his mother was still all-seeing. Brady only blushed and helped her arrange her pillows.

When he returned to the driveway, the girl was standing next to the pieces of the bicycle with the blow up beach ball she and the little boy had been kicking in her hands. She smiled at him. Her teeth were dazzling white and perfect. He actually felt himself go a little dizzy as he approached her.

"My brother's got quite a kick for a four year old!" she said. She propped the ball on her hip and extended her hand saying, "Hi. I'm Mary."

"Brady," he answered. He'd learned long ago that it was better to be a man of few words around pretty girls than to be a man who stuttered and stumbled over his tongue. He hoped his smile looked welcoming.

"We just moved here," she said. Her face grew pink as she added, "I guess that's obvious. But it's my mom, really. I'll be at college in the fall. I just agreed to come along and help with my brother for the summer. My parents just split. This is all new for him and with my mom's job at the hospital, we thought it would be easier for him to have someone he knows to hang out with this summer." She paused and looked across the street. The boy was pushing a toy car up and down the front steps of their house. "Gosh. I'm rambling," she said.

He nodded his head, wanting to tell her his story, too. He didn't want her to think that he was some loser kid just spending his summer at home, taking apart bicycles in front of his house for no apparent reason. But the truth of his situation put a lump in his throat that he couldn't seem to speak around. So instead he just nodded and tried to compliment her little brother's skill at kicking the beach ball and he couldn't stop noticing how the sunlight made a halo of her red hair around her finely freckled face.

About That Kiss
Mike Graves

Dear, Bea... About that kiss.

Miles had no idea what to write. About that kiss? He'd thought of little else but that kiss for the last forty-eight hours. Bea pounding her fists on her thighs. Bea lunging forward, throwing her arms around his neck, kissing him in public, and racing out the door. Miles hadn't seen Bea in the past two days, since the episode in the deli. He'd expected her to come to his office, but she hadn't shown. He thought he'd catch her after class, but she'd skipped his class today. Now it was Friday, and next week was a short one, just two days before the Thanksgiving break. Miles hated the thought of leaving for the break without having discussed this with Bea.

He didn't know how to reach her. He didn't have her phone number or address. He briefly considered using the school email, but quickly abandoned that idea. Too many horror stories of electronic missives going public. He didn't need that.

So Miles settled upon writing her a letter. He'd write a note, seal it in an envelope, and put it in her mailbox in the GTA office. He took a sip of his Americano and glanced at the other Starbucks patrons. A man and woman in the corner had their heads together, smiling as they pointed at a laptop computer screen. Three coeds sat on a couch laughing and talking and leaning toward a coffee table to pick at blueberry muffins and biscotti. Miles heard other people behind him, but didn't turn around. A man took a table next to Miles and reached into his book bag for a pad and pen. Miles recognized him as a GTA in his department, but he couldn't recall his name. Maybe he was going to write a letter, too, Miles thought. Maybe he was a poet. The barista yelled, "Grande latte for Calvin!" and the man left his table to get his drink.

Miles returned to his letter. About that kiss, Miles thought. About that kiss. That line from Princess Bride came to him and he smiled. "Since the invention of the kiss, there have only been five kisses that were rated the most passionate, the most pure. This one left them all behind." Right, Miles, you incurable romantic. Back to the letter.

First, let me say your kiss caught me by complete surprise. When you hinted in my office that we might share secrets, I thought you were just teasing me and being coy. Now this. I need to see you, Bea. I need to see you and talk to you. Are you teasing me? Was this a joke? A dare? Are you laughing at me or do you care for me? Don't hide, Bea. Don't hide. Come to me, please.

Miles didn't sign the letter. He folded it and sealed it inside an envelope. He leaned back and reached for his coffee. At the next table, the GTA, Calvin, also leaned back and reached for his coffee. The two men caught each other's eye and nodded hello.

So much for resolve, Miles thought. So much for my determination to focus on my work and not get distracted. Calvin, at the next table,

jerked his head toward the window. His mouth opened. Miles turned
to the window, but saw nothing unusual. Some students walking by.
Traffic on Bluemont Avenue. What had given Calvin a start? What
had he seen?

***

"I got your note."

Bea stood in the doorway. Miles smiled at her and motioned
toward a chair. Bea sat down, and they looked at each other across
the desk. It was Tuesday afternoon. A small pile of essays, waiting to
be corrected, rested next to a larger pile of graded papers. Miles had
about an hour of work to complete before locking the door and
heading south to Wichita for Thanksgiving with his parents. He'd
hoped to see Bea before the holiday. Now that she was here, he didn't
know what to say.

"I'm glad you're here, Bea. I wanted to see you."

Bea almost whispered.

"Yeah, that's what your note said."

"Look, Bea. I'm confused. You've been flirting with me, toying
with me, and then last week you kissed me in the deli. That was one
terrific kiss I might add. I felt it from my lips to my toes. So, what's
going on? Is this a game you're playing?"

Bea looked at her lap. When she looked up, her eyes were moist.

"Yes. No. I don't know."

"That's not much of an answer. I'm getting even more confused."

"I know, Miles, and I'm sorry. I guess I'm confused, too."

Miles picked up a fountain pen from his desk and pretended to
study its nib.

"Look, Bea. I want to tell you something about me. I was recently
in a relationship that ended suddenly. It still hurts. I promised myself
I wouldn't get involved in another relationship for a while. Then you
appear. You appear, and my head spins, and my stomach turns to
jelly. Please be honest with me, Bea."

Bea brushed her eyes with the back of her sleeve.

"I want to be honest, I really do. I haven't always been honest with
men, but I want to be honest with you."

Miles waited for her to continue.

"It started as a joke, a dare I guess. My sometime friend, Sally, put
me up to it. She dared me that I wouldn't kiss you. I told her I would.

I told her I would, and I said that if I kissed you, you'd kiss me back. So I did kiss you, Miles. I did kiss you, and when I did, you kissed me back. Only it wasn't just funny anymore. It wasn't just a joke anymore. I kissed you, and my head started spinning. My stomach turned to jelly. It was no longer just a dare. Suddenly, the joke wasn't on you. Suddenly the joke was on me."

Miles smiled.

"So why all the drama, Bea? We feel something for each other. That's good isn't it?"

"I want it to be good, but I want it to be honest, too. I was afraid you'd be angry with me. I haven't always been honest, Miles."

Bea looked into her lap again.

"You're being honest with me now. You started with a prank, and now we've ended up here. Can't we just see where this takes us?"

"I saw you the other day, Miles, and I wanted to talk to you, but I couldn't. You were sitting in Starbucks, and I was riding by on my bicycle."

"Why didn't you come in?"

"I told you I couldn't. Someone else was there. A ghost from my past. Someone I hadn't treated well. I saw him, and I saw you, and I saw myself. I saw a man I'd treated badly, and I saw a man I cared for and wanted to know, and I saw myself treating you badly, and I just couldn't stand it. I rode by."

"Bea, this is very confusing, but I do know this. I want to see you. I want to get to know you. Whatever happened in the past is past. Use the next few days to relax. Clear your mind. Come back after Thanksgiving and give us a chance."

Bea stood up, leaned over the desk, and gave him a peck on the cheek.

"Happy Thanksgiving, Professor Dude."

Miles touched his cheek as he watched her walk through the door.

Writers at K-State
Kevin Rabas

Julie didn't call or write or come by, and so Calvin wondered. He didn't call Bea. He read the books he had to read. He graded papers in purple ink. (It was K-State.) He wrote and wrote. Calvin started a book of starts, beginnings. A first stanza a day. He used that book to write the first few paragraphs of a story. He turned it in to show he wasn't lazy in one class when a novel didn't pan out. His professor didn't give the book of starts back. No matter. These were the things of his youth, his early work, he thought, he had to think, and move on. Calvin read Elizabeth Dodd, who knew her Nature, knew the prairie and its birds like no other, who knew Nature was nothing to compare your humans to; he read Holden, irreverent citizen of this world, who put bop wit into the meadowlark's throat; he read Heller, who knew Hawaii and its ghosts and how each man could be linked to the car he drove or wished to drive. And there were others, Doc Fedder, who could turn four words into a play, a way to start: once, however, but, so. And Cockinos, out with the prairie hawks, the talons and the thin purple tongue. Calvin remembered how he read Dodd and Heller in the K-State library during his campus visit. The books were on the university shelves, and he read quickly, thinking, I have a lot to learn. Calvin thought that he might write Julie a letter, a long letter, show her what was going on. Something might have happened. Or maybe his poems were not her thing. He'd said too much. He'd risk it, though. Say some more.

When Calvin went out his front door to get the mail there was that green bike, chained to the wooden railing of his small porch. Bea must be in Aggieville. Calvin lived three houses from the upper edge of Aggieville. But why would she leave the bike? Calvin recognized that he did not know the ways of women. He loved them. He sat down to tea, a boy in a girl's world, and he hoped to be able to follow all of the rules. He said what he felt. He tried on her life. He hoped to help, to be an accompanist of sorts, on brushes on snare drum, on piano, if he could keep up. He waited. He watched and held a hand. He kissed. His was a life of being the second one. But also he could shine, once in a while, solo across the keys, shine like a klieg light, like a sun, and say, Follow me. That moment in the light had not happened with Bea, and now, Calvin thought, it would never happen. She had gone. She'd left the stage, and here he was, alone, with nothing left to play.

Calvin looked out his front window. Bea's green bike shone like hot metal, like white fire, on his porch, the handlebars like the white tip of a fireplace poker, and he thought he might follow that bike, follow it back home, or he might turn and ignore its shine. Calvin got the claw hammer from out back. He pulled on the railing and pulled it apart. The chain slipped through, over and under the rust, the bent nails. Then he pushed the nails back down, the corner pieces of wood back into place, tapping it a few times with the head of the hammer. The bike was free again. It was hers and not hers. But it would never be his. He knew this. He'd rambled long enough on thoughts, but the thing, the bike, with it, he knew what to do. Leave it there. Take it, he thought. Take it back, somebody. Let her walk.

Calvin went back inside. He called Julie's number.

Chain Lady answered. "I'll give you her number," she said. "I think she likes you. She likes your poems, she says. Where do you get that, writing girls poems? Do you play flute, too?"

"It's what I do. What I came for. To learn how to write. Write well."

"If things don't work out with Julie, write me a poem, will ya?"

"What's Julie's number again?"

"Don't forget. I want a poem, if it doesn't work out. How come my guys don't write me poems? You tell me that."

"Do they like to read? Like to write?"

"No. They play in bands."

"I drum, too. But the retirement plan for musicians isn't so good. So, I write, too."

"Good thinking, poet-boy. Good thinking. I hear the retirement plans for poets aren't so good either."

"True. We teach. We teach and retire, and the writing. It's what we do when we're not grading and reading and talking in front of crowds of people. Crowds seated at desks."

"I hate public speaking. You can have it. And here's her number 816-357-2233. Good luck, poet-boy. You know, her daddy's rich. Good luck with him."

A Clean Green Bike

Tracy Million Simmons

It was beginning to feel like routine. Brady found himself rushing through the morning chores so that he could pull the flat of cardboard topped with all the pieces of his mother's bicycle out of the garage into the driveway. His mother would wave from the window on the days she was awake and Mary would arrive with her little brother in tow. The three of them would clean and polish bike parts until Colin, Mary's brother, grew tired of the task. Then they'd toss the beach ball, push toy cars down the driveway, and play games like hide and seek and freeze tag. Brady found it easy to entertain Colin. It made him feel good to remember what it was like to be four years old and to have so few complications in life.

One afternoon Colin and Brady ran around the yard playing policeman and bad guy while Mary curled on the ground in the shade of the maple tree and read a paperback novel. From the cover, Brady guessed it might be a love story. From the beating of his heart in his chest each time Mary smiled at him, Brady thought he might love the girl. She talked incessantly and he ached for the sound of her voice when she left his yard late each day.

Mary had more plans for the future than anyone he'd ever known. She had her college years mapped out, from completing her prerequisites early so that she could take a few "fun" classes in between, to the year she planned to study abroad and the list of companies to which she would dedicate summer internships. She even shared with him her notebook where she had planned her own major. It had something to do with women's studies and sociology and business, which Mary claimed would be ideal for her future work promoting women-owned businesses in underdeveloped countries.

His own plan of going to K-State and maybe majoring in accounting felt flat and entirely without direction next to hers.

It didn't stop Brady from hanging on Mary's every word, however. It didn't stop him from dreaming that she would change her mind about a private school in Minnesota and would announce, any day now, that she'd decided to stay in Manhattan where she could continue to care for her brother Colin. She could continue to spend her free time with Brady. They could go to school each day together, and in a couple of years, maybe, they'd even move out of their respective homes and get a place together, closer to campus.

Each evening Brady would tell Mary's plans and stories to his mother. At night, Brady would talk to his mother at least as much as Mary had talked to him throughout the day. It helped him commit her to memory. He didn't want to forget a single moment he spent with Mary.

His mom would listen quietly with her eyes closed. Sometimes she slept while Brady talked, and occasionally she would nod or say something like, "How nice," or "She sounds like a sweet girl." One day his mother said, "I'd really like to meet Mary some time."

That's why Brady didn't object a few days later when Mary

followed him into the house on one of his regular trips to check on his mother.

They hadn't really talked about his mother before. Brady had sort of mentioned that his mother was sick. He thought he'd said enough that Mary would understand the extent of his mother's illness, that she was not a woman who would miraculously recover and come running out of the house to try out her bicycle, should Brady ever get it back together again.

All the way up the stairs, Brady was aware of the heat of Mary's body so close to his as she followed. She was telling him about an article she'd read in a recent news magazine. He'd never interrupted her before, but when they reached his mother's door, he stopped and said, "Maybe you don't want to..." and Mary said, before he had a chance to finish, "But I do. I'd love to meet your mother. It's okay. It will be a good thing. I should meet her."

He took this to mean that maybe Mary loved him too. Why else would it be important that she meet his mother? What was good about Mary knowing his mom unless it was to be able to tell their children someday, "I met her, and she was a wonderful woman."

Brady hoped with every fiber of his being that his mother would be wonderful that day. He hoped this would be a day when she was alert and awake and would call Mary by name and be a gracious host, even from the confines of her deathbed.

His mother rallied as best she could. Sleep kept overcoming her between the words of her sentences, but she smiled at Mary and her eyes met theirs and only a couple of times did she open them and seem startled to find anyone there at all. Mary started taking turns with Brady; she would leave him with Colin and go check on his mother. They shared their burdens—little brother and sick mother—and to Brady it felt natural and completely right.

He began to put the polished and freshly green painted parts of the bicycle back together. Colin's pudgy little fingers would offer up pieces as Brady pointed to the next he needed. They would pause for races with Colin's toy cars. Together, he and Mary and Colin weeded his mother's flower gardens.

He called his father home when his mother's eyes grew dull. She began refusing meals. She drank water only sparingly. She slept for hours on end without ever waking. When Mary went home in the evening, Brady would sit by his mother's bed for hours, watching her chest rise and fall, wondering when he would witness her last breath.

On the day he finished rebuilding the bicycle, Mary kissed him. Not a romantic kiss on his lips, but he felt its significance all the same. The bicycle was ready and Mary threw her arms around him and pressed her warm lips against his cheek. She then threw her leg over the bike and pedaled down the driveway. Back and forth, up and down the road, they took turns trying out the bike.

That evening, his mother passed away.

A Picaresque Novel
Mike Graves

Miles sat on the couch facing the laptop propped on the coffee table. A mug of black coffee steamed beside the laptop. It was his third cup. Sunshine was breaking through the east window. He'd hoped to knock off a few pages before the others woke up. Miles was exploring the history surrounding the picaresque novel *Simplicius Simplicissimus*. He'd learned more about the Thirty Years War from reading the novel than he had in his undergraduate history classes.

"Good morning, Miles. Hard at it, eh? Atta boy."

His dad padded through the living room on the way to the kitchen for a cup of coffee. He was proud of Miles, proud of his intelligence and his diligence. His dad was a construction worker and admired hard work in others.

Miles found a good place to stop and powered down the computer. It would be difficult to concentrate with others milling around the house. Besides, Miles focused deeply when he worked, and he felt he should spend some time with his parents. He didn't have to write the paper. It would probably never be published. He planned on using it in the classroom. However, when he worked, he focused on the work. He avoided thinking about other things. He escaped life's complications. He didn't dwell on Bea. His dad returned to the living room with coffee.

"Quite a day yesterday. God, I ate too much. It was good to have everyone here, though."

Miles agreed. He hadn't seen his brothers in too long. They'd stopped by for the day with their families, but everyone left after dinner. People who didn't teach had to work the day after Thanksgiving.

"So, Son, tell me. How's the old love life? Seeing anyone you want the parents to meet?"

"Jeez, Dad."

"Oh, relax. What's a holiday at home without a few uncomfortable questions?"

Miles's mother came downstairs, sat down next to him, and gave him a hug. His dad nodded at the laptop.

"Miles is hard at it, honey. Looks like he's been up for hours. He's going places."

His dad stood up and stretched and went upstairs to dress. His mother smiled and squeezed his hand.

"Is that right, Miles? Have you been up for hours?"

"Well, I've been up for a while. You know me, Mom. I don't sleep well anyway, and I thought I'd work on a paper while the house was quiet."

"Your father is very proud of you, Miles. So am I."

She continued holding his hand while she spoke.

"That means a lot to me, Mom."

"So is this what 'publish or perish' means, Miles? You have to work on holidays?"

"Well, there is pressure, but I like to work when I can."

His mother sat silently, holding his hand, and looking at her son. Finally she spoke.

"What's troubling you, Miles?"

Julie's Dad
Kevin Rabas

Calvin dialed Julie. He wondered if this would be his last call. If she was avoiding him, this might be it.

"Julie. It's me. Chain—Your roommate gave me your number. I just wanted to call to see if you were—"

"It's my dad," Julie said. "He had another heart attack. We're in KC. I'm taking a few weeks break from school. To be here with him. I'm sorry we fell out of touch. I just had to go, and go right away. My dad needs me. I want to be here for him."

"Is he doing ok?"

"I think so. He's eating. He's a big man. Robust. He's barrel shaped or beach-ball shaped. He loves to eat. My mother, Ginny, used to cook and cook for him. She was part of a big Italian family, and we know how to cook. He just kept getting bigger and bigger. He never stopped. His heart, it can't keep up. That bloody motor, it wants to quit. So, it did. It conked out on him again. Calvin, I'm worried about him."

"I'm sure being there helps him. You're doing what you can. He loves you, and you're there out of love. For him."

"Do you love your parents, Calvin?"

"Yes. Very much. It's hard to say how much. My father suffered a breakdown last winter, and I went home to help. So, I might know a little about how you feel, what you're going through, just having to wait and be there, not being able to do anything but sit and wait."

"That's how it is. I'm glad you called. Let's get together when I come back. And someday maybe you'll meet my dad."

"Someday."

"I'll call you when I get back in Manhattan."

"Can I write you? Email?"

"I love your poems. Here's our address." Julie told Calvin she liked the idea of old fashioned correspondence. She didn't plan on using email, she said, except to turn in papers for school. She said she wanted him to write. Calvin knew that was what he could do, something he did well. He wondered if she'd be grading him, and would he have to slog through the compulsories first, as on ice, do the turns and spins before he could move up to the freestyle competition, before he could show her he could impress, had his own style, knew what to say when pressed. Would he come in at level one or level two? He knew this would be a hard time for her.

To Bea or Not to Bea
Mike Graves

"Hello, Miles."

And just like that, there she was, standing on his porch. It was Sunday evening, the Thanksgiving weekend was winding down, and Miles was unpacking. He hadn't been home long. He'd used the break to rest, to work, to spend time with his family, and most of all, to think. He'd spent some time alone, quiet time with just his thoughts, especially on the drives to Wichita and back. Miles needed to think, and he cherished his time alone. He'd thought about love, and he'd thought about Bea, and he'd thought about how his life would be if he let her into it. Would it work? Did she want to be a part of his life? Did he want her to be a part of his life? To Bea or not to Bea...

"What are you doing here?"

"I need to see you. Please let me come in."

Miles had thought about other things on the drive, too. Miles pretended that love, at least his love, was more than a glandular reaction to circumstances. He believed his mind trumped his hormones. He trusted his mind above all else and believed he'd make the right choice, believed he'd remain in charge of his life, fate be damned, if only he kept a cool head and thought things through. He pretended he was an existentialist on guard against the forces of romanticism. Think, Miles, think. That was his mantra.

"Do you think this is a good idea?"

"Please, Miles, I have things to say to you."

Now his thoughts tossed around in his head like straw in a Kansas wind storm. Nothing seemed clear. All that windshield time, all that time spent alone with his thoughts, seemed so irrelevant and long ago. What had been so crystal clear in his mind only an hour ago now seemed cloudy, blown back into the recesses of his mind. He wasn't aware that he'd pushed the door open and stepped back. He barely heard himself speak. He whispered.

"Sure. Come on in."

She smiled at him. Miles may have smiled back. She came through the door. Miles looked into her eyes and found his voice.

"How have you been, Wanda?"

***

Miles had a headache. An hour ago he'd been so certain, so confident. A knock on the door had changed all that. Thoughts in his mind that had been clear and ordered now lay in a heap like unsorted laundry. An hour ago he'd been sure. He'd made a decision. He knew what he wanted. He'd decided to ask Bea to come into his life, if she would have him. He still had doubts and fears. He didn't know where their journey would lead, but he wanted to begin the journey. He wanted to be with her. Then came that knock on the door and along with it a rush of painful memories—and pleasant ones. When Wanda knocked on his door, and when Miles let her in, resolve had washed away. Now Miles struggled to regain control and composure as he listened to Wanda's voice. She sat beside him on the couch.

"I've missed you, Miles. I've tried to deny it, I've tried to convince myself I'm over you, but I've missed you, Miles."

Miles listened. He didn't speak. He stared at the cover of *The New Yorker* he'd tossed on the table. The magazine's mascot, Eustace Tilley, peered through his monocle, his nose pointed upward. The dandy seemed to have all of the answers. At least he possessed an air of confidence. Miles did not. He tried to reorder his thoughts, his feelings. This wasn't right. This wasn't happening. Wanda had walked out on him. She'd crushed him. Now she wanted to come back?

Wanda leaned into Miles and put her lips next to his ear.

"I think about us, Miles. I think about our time together. I miss that passion, that heat. I want you."

She flicked his ear with her tongue. She squeezed his arm. Miles felt a rush of emotion, a flush of warmth. Was it love? He closed his eyes and recalled memories of their lovemaking. Wonderful, tender moments. Stolen moments. But was it love? Wanda's hand stroked his chest. He turned his head toward her, and their lips came together.

Miles drew back.

"Wanda, I don't think…"

Miles couldn't remember exactly how the next few minutes unfolded. Did he hear the knock at the door first? Did he draw back before hearing the knock? Wanda had her arms around him. He turned his head toward the door. He saw a shadow. A face? He uncurled from the couch and rushed to the door. No one was on the porch. He saw movement on the street. Under the streetlight a figure pedaled a bicycle. The bicycle was green.

Flying Wine
Kevin Rabas

"You unchained my bike," Bea said.

"I didn't think you wanted to be here," Calvin said.

Bea had come back, and she had some things to say.

"I found your nail polish remover and a few other things. They're in the…old wicker laundry basket. Please take them."

"I've been looking for that nail polish remover. Thanks."

Bea looked frazzled, and she'd been riding too long. Beads of sweat ran down her arms. Out of sorts, Calvin saw her in a new way. She must have been chasing something, Calvin thought, something she couldn't catch.

"I'm sorry for how things worked out," Bea said. "Come get your clothes sometime, will you? You know, I looked in the washer, and there they were, Calvin's clothes. I almost cried."

"It's ok, Bea. I've missed you, too."

"Got any wine?" Bea said.

Calvin brought two wine glasses and a bottle of red. After a few glasses, gesturing, Bea let her glass fly. Calvin got down on the carpet with a wet hand towel and worked to pull the red-purple stain from the tan.

"You know me," Bea said, "always losing my glass, when I'm happy."

"Are you happy?" Calvin said.

"I think I am."

Calvin and Bea Cook, 30
Kevin Rabas

"Let's cook something together, Calvin," Bea said.

Calvin's mother didn't let him touch anything in the kitchen as a kid, and he lived at home most of undergrad. Now, two hours away from home, he slowly bought more and more food—cans and brightly-colored packages—and grouped them by country in the glass -door cabinets. He had Asia (with soba noodles, rice, hoisin sauce, and green wasabi in a tube), Italian (with three kinds of noodles and two varieties of premade red sauce, along with two little cans of tomato paste and one big can of tomato sauce to make his own, along with basil and oregano), soups (tomato, beef stew, Italian wedding, Matzo balls with broth), Middle Eastern (dried apricots, chick peas, spices), and so on. Bea said that when she first visited Calvin's place she thought he was a cook or chef, seeing all of that food.

Calvin took down the chickpeas and dried apricots. He scored a red onion, then showed the result to Bea. She approved. He sliced it, near the top, one big ring, then another, that fell into square pieces. Bea joined in, cutting the apricots into slices. Calvin sautéed onion and garlic, then put water and chick peas in to boil in the sauce pan. He took canned tomatoes down from the shelf and three fresh tomatoes.

Bea said, "Are you going to be famous by 30?"

"I don't know," said Calvin. "Do I need to be?"

"I want a writer who hits by 30. Can you do it?"

"What's riding on it?"

"Me."

"I think I can do it. Want to stick around and see?"

"There is someone else."

Calvin left it at that. After they ate, a warmth came over them both, and Bea stood and gave Calvin a long hug.

"I must go," she said.

"I know. You've got someone else. I may, too."

"I like how we understand each other. We're like old people. I look, and you don't say anything, but just pass the pepper, knowing."

Bea got on her green bike and pedaled into the night. Calvin didn't feel sad, but he felt empty. He ate some more apricot chickpea dinner, then he put away the rest of it in the fridge. Maybe Julie would like some when she returns. He took some out of the Corningware bowl and put it into a smaller, disposable Tupperware bowl with a tight lid, and he froze it. Calvin wasn't too worried about what would happen. Bea would come and go, now, he knew it. Besides, Bea never liked Julie. One time, after a party that had gone wrong, she said, "You'll leave me for someone I hate, one day. Julie, maybe. You like her." Calvin said nothing. And he wasn't about to tell her about Julie now. Timing was everything. Calvin took out his brushes and made circles on his snare drum. He turned on Miles Davis's "Kind of Blue" album and played until it was completely dark out the window. Then, he got out his books and read. He'd write, when he could read no more. He might start on that letter to Julie. He might write a poem. He was 22. He had a few years before 30 was upon him. He wondered if Bea would come back then. They'd made a kind of pact in that moment, unknowingly. Calvin wondered what it all meant, what it all might bring.

A Married Woman

Mike Graves

Miles leaned back in his chair with a student essay in his hand. He glanced at the remaining pile of essays on his desk and then at the clock. It would be a long afternoon. The essays were good, not great but good. Miles had completed his paper on the historical events surrounding the novel, *Simplicius Simplicissimus*, and he'd used his work as a theme for his students' essays. Maybe a diligent young scholar would uncover a new twist in the seventeenth century picaresque novel. One could hope. He'd read three essays with ten to go when she came into his office. He tossed the essay he was holding onto his desk and gestured toward the chair. She sat down and stared into her lap. Neither spoke right away. Miles broke the silence.

"I'm glad you came, Bea. I have a lot to tell you."

Bea nodded but didn't speak, so Miles continued.

"That was you who knocked on my door Sunday night, wasn't it?"

She nodded again.

"I thought so. Listen, Bea, what you saw isn't what you think it is. The woman who was with me is an old friend. We had a thing once, but it ended. It's over. Actually, she ended it first, and I ended it again Sunday night. I told her it was over. It is, Bea. It's over. I hope you believe me."

Bea sat still for a moment before looking up.

"I know her, you know. I know who she is. One of my ex-boyfriends is a buddy of her husband. If her husband ever found out, he'd shoot you."

Miles knew Bea was right. And if one person knew, soon another one would, then another, and so on. How did everything get so complicated?

"Look, Bea, I'm not proud of having an affair with a married woman, but I did it. All I can do is promise you it is over and behave better in the future. Can we talk about us?"

"Us, Miles? Is there an 'us'? What makes you think there is an 'us'? All I did was kiss you."

Miles took off his glasses and rubbed his eyes with the tips of his fingers.

"I know it was just a kiss, Bea, but I thought you were telling me something. I thought you were saying you wanted more. There are kisses, and there are kisses."

"Yeah, well, I don't know what I'm feeling now. I haven't always been honest with my boyfriends, and like you I want to behave better in the future. I'm attracted to you, Miles, but I haven't sorted out my feelings. I may just be infatuated. Meanwhile, there is another man I used to date."

Bea looked into her lap again.

"I treated him badly, and I feel terrible about it. I'm not sure if that relationship is over."

Miles put his glasses back on.

"Look, Bea, I don't know where this is headed either. Let's just be honest with each other. I'm sure my relationship is over. I want to spend some time with you. Let's leave it at that for now, okay? Come to me when you can, if you can."

Bea nodded and stood up. She smiled but didn't speak. Miles watched her walk through the door. He glanced at the clock on the wall and the papers on his desk. It was going to be a long afternoon.

Calvin and Ceramics Studio, Writing Julie
Kevin Rabas

Calvin put the nail polish remover back under the bathroom sink. Bea had forgotten it again. She'd come back. He walked down to the old stadium. Beneath it was the ceramics studio. Young men and women hunched over kick wheels here. A metal circle spun, and you used that spinning wheel to defy gravity, to make clay rise. Attached to the wheel was a long rod that ran almost to the floor. Near the floor, the rod attached to a rock wheel about four feet in diameter. You hunched on a tractor seat and you kicked that rock wheel that spun the metal wheel above, and you used your hands to push and pull and delicately shape the clay. Calvin wasn't much good at it. He went to remember Julie, to think of her.

A young woman with purple hair and headphones on was pulling a pot upward into a long, cylindrical vase. It was about three feet tall now, had thick sides, and might go higher. She had strong hands. She looked at Calvin and nodded, but didn't much care if he was there.

A woodsy guy with dreadlocks and small hands pulled clay into a small gourd-like jar, then took it off the wheel and carved into it with a scalpel tool and stick. The script looked like cuneiform or Egyptian Sanskrit. He lit up a stogie and asked Calvin if he wanted to smoke. A breeze went through the studio, in through the stadium and out through the studio doors. Calvin said no, but he watched the smoke go. Like a spirit, it went. Sometimes the smoke hovered over the clay pot, over the words, like the breath of God.

Calvin sat at one of the wheels and wrote on a yellow legal pad. He wrote in pen quickly. He wrote to Julie:

I walked down to the studio today, thinking you might be here,

knowing you wouldn't be. Every hand covered in clay

could be your hand. But none were. I watched the clay cover

the hands, like river mud, like a caress, more like water

than like mud, and I think about a time when I might

take your hand and hold it, hold it the way water does or clay does,

gently, the hold of liquid, the hold of spirit, the hold of smoke,

almost like it isn't there, but never letting go, leaving

some of itself with you, like the faint taste of a sweet kiss.

Calvin didn't know if this was taking it too far. He'd look at it again later. For now, he had something. He'd go back to his reading, he thought. This evening it was *Modern American Poetry*. He was reading Mina Loy, her butterfly with the news written in blood on its wings. More than a surrealist, she knew love, Calvin thought, how it was beautiful, but also full of darkness. How communion with someone was like communion with God, with a Creator, and also like the touch and shadow of death. How else would we see it, feel it? Touch gently, he thought. There is little else, Calvin thought, love and art.

The Ones That Got Away
Mike Graves

Miles sat at a small table in the Aggieville Starbucks facing a blank sheet of paper. He'd turned the table slightly so he wouldn't be distracted. Ahead of him a burnt orange wall and a forest green wall came together. He stared at the juncture and thought of Little Jack Horner.

Thoughts came rapidly, and he tried to slow them down, to focus on one or two at a time. He thought about his recent visit with his brothers at Thanksgiving and how they'd regaled the family with their hunting exploits. His brother Randy had wounded a pheasant, and the bird had tried to run. He should have let Sissy, their black lab, run down the bird, but instead he had fired another load of buckshot into it. Everyone found great humor in this.

"That bird was so full of buckshot it rattled when we picked it up," his other brother, Don, said with laughter. "Anyone who takes a bite into that rooster will most assuredly break a tooth."

The rest of the family laughed, but Miles only grinned. He'd hunted in the past, but had finally concluded he found little pleasure in the sport. He loved stomping through the woods. He loved the sounds his boots made on the crisp stubble in the fields. He loved the sharp, cold smells of earth, and hunting dogs, and his wool scarf. He just didn't see the point in spoiling it all by shooting birds and animals.

Miles wrote a line on his paper:

> Somewhere where men gather,
>
> to brag and shout and boast.

He thought about women he'd known, women he'd cared for, women he still cared for. He recalled his first girlfriend. He was in the sixth grade, and the family lived on the east coast. His class took a weekend field trip to Washington, D.C., an overnighter. He sat on the bus next to Tommy, his best friend, but he kept watching and listening to Debbie who sat on the seat ahead of them. Once in a while she turned around and smiled at him. Before the weekend was over, Miles had given Debbie a gift, a set of three turquoise and silver bracelets. The bracelets cost only a couple of bucks, all he had in his wallet, and of course, they were cheap imitations. In only a few weeks they left rust marks on Debbie's wrists, but she didn't take them off. She kept wearing them. That simple gesture tore at Miles's eleven-year-old heart.

He wrote another line. From across the room a barista called out a name, but Miles paid no attention. He sat back and gnawed at the tip of his Waterman fountain pen. Stephen King had once commented that the Waterman fountain pen was the best word processor he'd ever used.

Miles recalled an unpleasant event from high school. The junior varsity football team was in the locker room, and Chris Wills was holding court. Chris had gone out with Sandy Baker the night before, and they'd gone all the way. Now Chris was sharing all of the details. Miles was only fourteen at the time, years away from his first experience with a woman, as were most of the other boys. The other boys listened and hooted, but Miles edged away to his locker and dressed quietly. His stomach was upset, and he just wanted to dress and leave.

He wrote another line.

He thought about Wanda. He thought about Bea. Wanda had given him up. When she'd tried to come back, he'd given her up. What about Bea? There was someone else in her life. Had he lost her before they'd given each other a chance?

Miles wrote another line. He read what he wrote, changed a word here and there, and read it again. Was it any good? He didn't know. Truthfully, he didn't really care. It spoke to him. He raised his Americano to his lips and read one last time.

The Ones That Got Away

Somewhere where men gather

to brag and shout and boast

about the ones they've landed

and the ones that fought the most,

I sit alone in a corner

apart from noise and fray

and lift my glass in silence

to the ones that got away.

Calvin Sends His Letter to Julie
Kevin Rabas

Calvin wrote more lines to Julie:

I remember you coming by my place. My mother said your mother sent

you, said we should meet, and you came to my door. How romantic. But

when I saw you I knew our mothers must have known something, known

something about how some puzzle pieces just fit, right away, the right ones in

the right places, and the puzzle completes around them. That was the way of it. I saw you and knew: She might be that missing part of me. I might complete her. It was something in your eyes, how they caught light, and you were uncommonly joyful, full of mirth and peace, a look I see when I see the Dali Lama on TV, that kind of uncontained happiness and peace, but with an energy the saintly, red-robed man does not have, and a mischievousness completely beyond him. Not that he too doesn't play tricks. I don't know you or don't know you well yet, but I hope to. I know you'll return with a dark cloud, a vision of your father with you, him in a hospital bed, white walls, whitewash all around him, and him, immobile, waiting, his chest rising, waiting for the body to heal. But know that the future also is with us, our moments among Kanza prairie and tallgrass, our moments under November sun. They await us. All we have to do is step into them, together, perhaps hand in hand.

Calvin put the letter in with the ceramics studio poem, closed the envelope, and placed it in the rusty black mailbox on his front porch that looked like an over-sized envelope with a metal flap at the top. He hoped Julie got his letter before she got home. He hoped she had some time think about what he had written. He hoped she'd come back and come into his life and extend one hand. He prayed for sun that day, that day she returned to home to Manhattan and perhaps came home to him.

Calvin Ponders His Solo, Undergrad Years
Kevin Rabas

In undergrad, his friends had called him the Monk. He didn't date. He didn't party. He didn't see many women. Perhaps he was now making time up. Calvin worked at the school paper, the *U-News*, and was always there. Thursday through Sunday, when not in class, he was in the newspaper building, a poorly renovated house with cracks from floor to ceiling on all the walls.

Calvin didn't sleep much. One night, when he did drift off on the *U-News* couch, a police woman woke him. She said, "Who are you?"

Calvin explained that he worked for the paper and was working late. And she said someone had come in the window and taken a computer and gone out the front door. Calvin hadn't noticed. He'd slept through it. "It doesn't look like you did it," she said. "Go home. Get some sleep," and she left. Calvin was on deadline. He stayed.

Calvin was Arts & Entertainment Editor. He went to art openings, the university opera performance, the ballet. He interviewed visiting artists. At one opening held in the Linda Hall Library, Calvin was wined and dined as he waited. A crowd ate shrimp on fancy crackers, gawking and talking around an emerald fountain. Calvin spread some thick black jelly on a piece of miniature toast. It tasted salty.

"What is it?" he'd asked the photographer. "That's a lot of caviar for one man," she said. He'd never had it before. Just how many dollars did he eat in one bite?

Culture came slow for Calvin. He'd grown up in a suburb of Kansas City, but not into wealth. His father was a construction worker, and his mother was a reporter for a small local paper. They kept him out of the good schools, saying, "We don't want you to grow snotty." He grew. Eventually, he grew to appreciate finer things.

Bea was cultured. Nudes hung on her walls, all women. Priestesses and Arthurian maidens and models and artist's muses, women in love with love and unafraid of being in love. Klimt and Toulouse-Lautrec, Waterman and Manet.

Julie was an artist, came from money, it appeared, but was new rich. Her appreciation seemed tactile and new in ceramics. Her hands knew what to do. But Calvin didn't see any art that wasn't her own on her walls. Julie also liked figure drawing. He'd seen the nudes, drawn in red charcoal, on the walls in her house. She was good. This WAS an artist, not an aficionado. She would grow, like Calvin did, into the culture, into the tribe. Calvin thought he might help her. Maybe she'd help him. He'd write her tonight.

Bea Wavers
Mike Graves

"Bea, it's good to see you. I've been thinking about you."

Miles grinned and kept talking.

"In fact, I haven't thought about much else. How are you, Bea? I hope you're well. Every time I see you in class, I want to talk to you, and it's been difficult not being able to. You look terrific. How have you been? What have you been thinking? Have you thought about us?"

Miles stopped talking. He smiled at Bea, and she smiled back. He was suddenly aware that he was prattling like a schoolboy. Bea undid her scarf and sat down at the table.

"It's good to see you, too, Miles. You look well. Yes, I've thought about you. I've thought about a lot of things. I've thought about you... and me. I've thought about us, and I've thought about other things."

Miles wondered what "other things" might be. A part of him knew or at least suspected. It had been a couple of weeks since they'd spoken together. November had slid into icy December. North winds bit through coats and jeans as students and teachers walked stiff-legged across campus, hunched over and unsmiling. Final exams loomed ahead, and faces grew serious, brows furrowed.

Bea had been attending his class, but in body only. Her mind had been elsewhere. She sat silently, took a few notes, did her assignments, but mentally she'd been absent. Now she was here, and for the first time in weeks, they would talk. They sat at a table in the deli. The deli, of course, was the place where Bea had kissed Miles in what seemed like a lifetime ago. Bea had arranged the meeting with a crumpled note stuffed into Mile's office mailbox.

"I won't ask you about the other things, Bea. I'll let you tell me in your own time, but please tell me your thoughts about us."

Bea stared at the spoon in her hand and twirled it slowly.

"Here's the thing, Miles. I'm attracted to you. I want to see you. I want to spend time with you. I think you're a nice man, and I'd like to be with a nice man."

Miles waited for more, but nothing came.

"So what's the problem? I want to see you, too."

"The problem is that there's somebody else. Someone I've known for a long time, and I'm not sure it's over."

Miles didn't like her reply, but he appreciated her honesty.

"So you've decided to stay with him, at least for now?"

She looked into his eyes.

"I don't know. I think I want to stay with him, but I'm not sure he wants to be with me. I think he may have found someone else. I don't know. I'm confused, Miles."

Miles processed this information.

"I've got to tell you this leaves me feeling a bit chilly. It sounds like you prefer this other guy, but if he won't have you maybe I've got a shot. Is that what I am, Bea? Am I your fallback position? Am I the guy you'll come to when your other life doesn't work? If that's the case, Bea, I'm not sure we should get involved."

Bea's eyes grew moist. She did not want to cry. She dabbed at her eyes with a napkin.

"No, Miles. Don't talk like that. You're not a second choice. I just can't make a choice. I'm not even sure I have a choice. God, I feel terrible."

Miles sat for a moment before speaking. He reached into his wallet and dropped a few bucks on the table.

"This isn't good. You're not ready. This isn't a good time. Exams are coming up, and we're both going to be busy. I care for you, Bea, but I care for myself, too. I don't want either of us to make the wrong choice. Take more time and talk to me again later."

Miles stood up, and Bea looked up at him. Neither of them smiled. Bea dabbed at her eyes, and Miles walked out the door.

Julie Returns, Lake

Kevin Rabas

Calvin fell asleep, his thick black anthology of *Modern American Poetry* on his chest. He was reading Wallace Stevens, wondering why there was a dead woman under a sheet while the homeowners set up camp out front and handed out ice cream, but he hadn't slept in hours, and no answers came, only images and dreams. He'd read the whole morning and most of the afternoon, and now, at 3, as the light of winter started in the window in blues and whites, yellows and golds, his eyelids slid, his head fell back, and he slept. He saw Julie. She was driving her white Mercury fast. The red stripe down the sides of the car blurred like a red lightning bolt speeding beside the car, an escort, a divine escort. Zeus's bolt beside her. She sped and sped, through red lights, through green lights. She raced towards Manhattan, not angry or frantic, but like a race car driver, because she was in love with speed.

Calvin heard thunder and awakened. No, it was knocking. He jumped up, the book fell in a heap, its pages splayed like an overturned glass. He went to the door, and there was Julie. She sparkled.

"I loved your letter. I thought I'd come by. Want to go to Tuttle (Creek Lake)?" She pointed to her car. The moon roof was open. The windows were all down. It was chilly, but it was Indian summer. She had on a coat with white fur at the neck, at the hood, but her coat was open. She didn't mind the chill.

"So good to see you, Julie," Calvin said. He grabbed his coat, a tan barn jacket. He tapped Julie on the shoulder, a light touch. He'd never touched anyone this way, but he was too shy to hug her. "How's your dad?"

"He's been better. But really he's ok. He told me to go and do something crazy. To forget about him for a day. So, I'm here. Want me to pick up Chain Lady on the way?"

"No," said Calvin, and they went.

A Flight or Two
Mike Graves

The red wine sparkled in its stemmed glass. It was an inexpensive burgundy, what the French refer to as "rough" wine, but it suited both his palate and his pocketbook. Miles took a sip and leaned back in his overstuffed chair. He listened to the sultry voice of Norah Jones croon about New York City, such a beautiful place. New York City, the real Manhattan. Miles wondered how life would be different if he lived in the Big Apple rather than the little one in north central Kansas. He closed his eyes and fantasized about the energy, the crowds, the bookstores, Broadway, the lights, living in a city that never sleeps. New York was his favorite city, and he wished he could afford to visit it more often. The last time he'd traveled to New York, the twin towers were still standing.

Exam week was winding down. He had one more exam to give and a stack of papers to grade, but he left the office that afternoon wanting nothing more than a quiet evening at home. He had a light supper and settled into his chair. He opened a copy of Jim Harrison's *Dalva*, and his thoughts drifted from his favorite city to the plains of Nebraska, the state Harrison declared was America's most beautiful. He read for only a few minutes before a knock announced a visitor.

"Hello, Bea."

Bea's face peeked from inside her red wool scarf and hooded parka.

"Hello, Miles. May I come in?"

"Sure."

Miles held open the door. While Bea took off her coat and got settled, he poured wine into another glass. They each sipped before Bea broke the silence.

"Miles, I've been thinking. If you're willing to go slow, I'd like to spend some time with you. I feel something for you, something strong, and I want to see where it takes me. That is, if you feel the same."

Miles smiled.

"Of course, Bea. I've been hoping for this. What about your other relationship?"

"I still feel something for him, but it's dying. It is for him, too, I think. In fact, I saw him with another woman today, riding around in her car."

"Is that why you're here, Bea? Because you feel rejected? Are you on the rebound and looking for me to catch you?"

Bea shook her head.

"No. That's not it. I care about you, Miles. I have for some time. I'm just being honest. There is, was, someone else. That's why I want to go slow. I don't want to rush into anything."

"Fair enough, Bea. Slow it is. What would you like from me?"

Bea put down her glass and moved closer to Miles.

"Miles, what I need now more than anything is a hug. Would you hug me?"

Miles smiled at her.

"Of course I'll hug you, Bea."

And he did.

***

Miles stepped onto the porch and noticed the green bicycle leaning against the steps. Its chain looked a little loose, and spots of rust were forming on the handlebars. He smiled.

"That old Schwinn has rolled into and out of my life many times in the last few months."

He held his car keys in his hand and had a sudden thought.

"Why not?"

He climbed on the bike and pedaled toward campus. A north wind blew, but rather than chilling him the brisk breeze brought him alive.

He pedaled faster and breathed in great lungs full of air. It would have taken more than a cool wind to dampen his spirits this particular morning.

Bea had stayed for most of the evening. They'd chatted and cuddled and finished the bottle of wine. They held hands and talked about everything and nothing. They each had traditional holiday plans. Miles would spend Christmas with his folks in Wichita, Bea with her family in Kansas City. They'd love to travel, but money was tight. They talked until it grew late. When Bea said she had to leave, Miles didn't want her to ride her bike in the frosty night. He drove her home in his Chevy Cavalier.

Now Miles rode the bike onto campus. He faced the final day of the semester. He rolled the bike into the rack and headed for his office. He had one more exam to give that morning and a number of papers to grade.

He didn't cross paths with Bea all day, but she filled his thoughts. He felt like he was running on autopilot. He gave his last exam, graded the stack of papers on his desk, and submitted final grades on his computer. Throughout the day, a few students drifted into his office, shared holiday greetings, asked about his plans, and hoped he'd mention their grades. An occasional student dropped all pretense of well-wishing and pleaded for leniency. Miles was taken by how ordinarily casual students would turn serious and scholarly toward the end of the semester.

Fred Holland stuck his head in the door.

"They're serving eggnog and cookies in the lounge."

"Thanks, Fred. I'll be along."

Fred frowned.

"No brandy in the eggnog, though. It's just that sweet, gloppy stuff."

Miles smiled and shook his head as Fred headed back to the lounge for seconds. He clicked his computer mouse to sign off and paused. He stared at the screen with his hands poised over the keyboard. He tapped some keys. An image of William Shatner/Captain Kirk/Denny Crane came up inviting him to name his own price on a hotel. He tapped a few more keys and shuddered. How could it cost that much to fly to San Francisco? He tried New Orleans. The cost was even higher. Everyone wanted to go south in the winter. Maybe someplace north might be reasonable. He tried New York City, but saw at a glance he couldn't afford it.

Come on, Kirk, show me something reasonable.

Miles tapped again. Whoa. This didn't look bad. He tapped again. Shatner struck a karate chop pose. Yes! It wasn't the Big Apple, but it was great. Miles reached for the phone.

"Bea, how would you like to go on a trip?"

Bea laughed.

"I'd love to, Miles. Is this your idea of taking things slow?"

Miles laughed, too. They talked for a few minutes and hung up. Miles turned back to the computer. A few final taps on the keyboard, and it was done.

The next morning Miles and Bea boarded an American Airlines flight bound for the nation's capital.

Mary Visits
Tracy Million Simmons

He didn't know how she'd gotten into the house. He didn't know if his father had opened the door for her and let her in, or if she'd found the key under the rock in his mother's flower bed, or if they simply hadn't locked the door at all after the hospice nurse left and the hearse rolled away with his mother's body.

Brady had showered and crawled into his bed, unable to imagine what sort of dreams might come. He'd barely pulled the covers to his chin when she'd knocked softly on his bedroom door and immediately entered without his answer. The street light through his bedroom window lit up her face for a moment. He marveled at the sparkle of her red hair, and then she was standing next to his bed and then on the bed alongside him, on top of the covers, but stretching her body the length of his, none-the-less.

"I'm so sorry," Mary whispered, her chin pressed against his shoulder. "You okay?"

She threw her arm across his chest and pulled her body closer to his.

"Yeah," Brady managed to say. "It's okay."

He didn't really know that it was okay, of course. He didn't feel what he expected to feel. He thought that maybe he was numb and in shock and it just hadn't hit him yet. He had imagined himself breaking down and crying over his mother's dead body. He imagined dropping to his knees and wailing the way people sometimes did in movies. He thought he might shout out to god, "Why? How could you?"

But what he felt when he'd stepped into his mother's room that evening, to find his father sitting there in silence, it was more relief than grief. It was almost as if her lack of breath had given him room to breathe deeper. It was as if a weight had been lifted from his chest, something physical that had been holding him down that he hadn't even realized was there. He thought that maybe he should feel guilty for the relief that he felt. He thought that having Mary beside him like this, her body pressed up against his, even with his blanket between their bodies, might be muddling his mind even more.

"I wish I had known her before she was sick," Mary whispered. "Tell me. What was she like?"

Brady thought for a moment, his eyes staring straight up at the ceiling. He dared not look at Mary. Her face was so close he could feel her breath on his ear. He was pretty sure they were close enough that their lips would meet if he turned his head. He wasn't sure that this was the time or the place for their first real kiss.

"She was always busy," he said. He pictured his mother in the kitchen and the way she simply couldn't stand for idle time, for instance waiting for something to heat on the stove. She'd stir a couple of times and then flit to the dishwasher where she might unload the top rack before distracting herself with a spot on the counter. She'd notice the dust on fan blades on her way to the cabinet for seasoning and she would pull over a chair and give them all a quick swipe before reminding herself that she'd been meaning to add chocolate chips to the grocery list. "She was a happy busy. Like a hummingbird. Here and there, and here again."

Mary was still with listening, and he found the words continuing.

"She had this idea that drinking wine could be romantic and healthy. She was always deciding she should drink more wine. She'd come home with a couple of different bottles, trying them out. She was always looking for a wine that was just the right amount of sweet."

Mary laughed lightly.

"She wasn't like, an alcoholic or anything. Far from it, really. It was like she had this idea that drinking wine was a grown-up sort of habit that she should develop, but she just couldn't stand the taste of it. She was more into stuff like chocolate milk or freshly squeezed lemonade."

"She loved riding that bike. She rode it all over town. She was always scolding my dad for driving places that were within riding distance." And that's when he felt it arrive. The grief stuck in his throat just a bit and he swallowed hard and had to blink back tears.

Mary just squeezed him tighter and they were together there in the silence until the wave passed and he felt himself able to breathe again.

"More?" she asked.

"She liked grapes in her tuna salad. She loved the movie, *The Wizard of Oz*. And she was always singing that Kermit the frog song."

"It's not easy being green?" Mary asked.

"No, about the rainbow," he answered, and sort of let himself sing it. "Why are there so many songs..." This brought the grief to the surface again. It threatened to choke him, but he pushed through it. "...about rainbows and what's on the other side." His voice cracked.

Brady closed his eyes and waited for this wave to pass, as well.

"She would have been totally not cool about you being here. A girlfriend in the bedroom. That's just asking for trouble," he said.

Mary laughed again lightly. "A friend," she said. "I think she would have understood. You're in need, and I'm a friend."

Brady smiled, just in case she could see his face by the glow of the street light that always cast pale shadows throughout his room, but her words made his heart ache in an entirely different way.

The National Mall
Mike Graves

Miles and Bea spent the afternoon walking the National Mall. They didn't have a plan, and Bea wondered how they'd see everything in one trip. Miles laughed and assured her there was no way to see it all.

"We'll see what we can, Bea. We only have a few days."

He paused and held her face in his hands.

"Maybe this is just the first of many trips."

Bea smiled, and they relaxed. They strolled. Sparkling, oversized flakes of snow wafted in the air. The winter weather was more peaceful than cold. The holiday season had sent most residents of D.C. home, and what was often a crowded city was busy, but not too busy. Tourists walked together in small groups speaking Japanese, Chinese, Italian and other tongues. A large number of visitors spoke French.

Miles and Bea decided to walk to the west end of the Mall. They took pictures of each other on the steps of the Lincoln Memorial. They stood silently at the Vietnam Veterans Memorial, its ebony walls rising and falling before them. An elderly gentleman wept as his trembling fingers brushed an engraved name on the wall. They left the Mall and walked north.

A Thai restaurant near the White House looked appealing.

"Do you like spicy food, Bea?"

"Love it."

"I knew we were meant to be together."

They shared an order of Miang kham, a delicious appetizer of meat, peppers, and vegetables wrapped in spinach leaves. They also had Phat phak kana mu krop, fried rice served with broccoli, red peppers, and soy sauce. Their waitress smiled each time she refilled their glasses. Bea's eyes were watering, but she laughed.

"This is testing my love for spicy food."

Miles took a big drink of water.

"I agree."

Bea reached across the table, and Miles rested his hand on hers. They were silent for a moment. The waitress interrupted them to ask about dessert. They declined and settled on coffee instead. They continued touching hands. A little bell above the door clanged when a man and a woman came in. The couple spoke German and took a table near the window. Bea squeezed Miles's hand.

"I don't know where this is headed, but I'm so happy you asked me to come on this trip."

"I'm happy you came."

"We haven't talked about the sleeping arrangements, Miles."

Miles had made reservations at the L'Enfant Plaza Hotel a couple of blocks south of the Mall. They'd dropped their bags off at the hotel when they arrived in D.C., but their rooms hadn't been ready so they'd decided to tour first.

"I promised you I'd go slowly, Bea. I've made reservations for two rooms. I won't pressure you."

Bea smiled and squeezed his hand again.

"No pressure, Miles. One room will be fine."

Miles returned her smile and looked at his watch.
"I'll bet our room is ready."
They both laughed. Miles paid the waitress, and they left.

Julie and Calvin Kiss at the Lake
Kevin Rabas

When Julie down-shifted into fourth gear, Calvin put his hand gingerly on top of hers. "Good. Keep it there," she said, and together they shifted into third and second. Soon, they coasted to a stop. Julie parked and set the brake. She reached over and pecked Calvin on the cheek. "I've wanted to do that for days," she said. "I think you're cute. And sweet. And you called."

They clasped hands and walked down to the waterside.

Calvin and Julie sat on some large rocks and held hands, and Calvin said, "So good you're back, and here, with me" and started a kiss, which was sweet, and held Julie, and her breath came like quick heaves, and her breasts felt like two doves against him, held but fluttering.

They walked the waterside, and Calvin spotted a rock that looked like a heart and gave it to Julie. "Is it an omen?" said Julie.

"I don't know if I believe in omens," Calvin said. "But for you, I might. I might believe in them, just once."

"It's too good to be true," Julie said, and threw the rock into the lake, and Calvin skipped rocks after it.

"Show me how," Julie said, and Calvin took her small hand—she was petite—and showed her how to fling the rock, to flick it like a Frisbee, hand almost parallel to the water. Julie leaned back against him as she threw, and he held her.

When they broke, Julie showed Calvin how to place his two hands like holding an invisible basketball and feel the energy go from one thumb, and one set of fingers, to the other, the energy moving, silent, hot, through the air.

"I learned it in Tai Chi," she said. "Can you feel the chi?" She watched him. Calvin caught her eyes on his. She took his hands in hers, and it was as if dusk came to them in that moment; the sky darkened around their hands and faces, and he was hers.

An Encore Performance
Mike Graves

They spent their first night in Washington, D.C. in their hotel room, snuggled in luxurious linens and pillows strewn across a king-sized bed. When they returned to the hotel, Miles stopped at the desk and changed their reservations from two rooms to one room, listed as a Superior View King. From the window they could see the Washington Monument. The brightly lit skyline sparkled at night.

Miles stood by the window watching Bea unpack her bag. Like Miles, she traveled light, a few clothes, a book or two, and a journal stuffed into a backpack. He appreciated her simplicity. In spite of their opulent surroundings, Miles leaned toward black coffee, blue jeans, fountain pens, and an inexpensive watch with a sweep second hand. It was delicious to share a deluxe room with a stunning view, but this was a getaway, playacting.

They'd shared only a few words since arriving at the hotel. Tension pressed on each of them, and they pretended to act casual. Their inevitable, forthcoming lovemaking remained unspoken and weighed on their minds. Miles took the initiative.

"You know what I'd like? I'd like an encore performance."

Bea wrinkled her brow.

"An encore performance?"

"Yes, an encore performance starring that crazy woman in the deli, the one who threw herself at me and clamped on a lip lock that tingled my toes and made me weak in the knees. I want to see that woman again."

Bea laughed and ran across the room. She wrapped her arms around his neck and drew his head down to hers. Their lips met. Bea kissed Miles, and he kissed her back, and they smiled. The tension was gone. They kissed and nibbled and laughed and fell onto the bed holding each other.

"That's what I call an encore."

"How about a new play?"

"Ladies and gentlemen…"

"Opening night…"

"A romance..."

"...starring Miles and Bea..."

"in a long run…"
"…with lots of curtain calls."
"Encore!"
"Applause!"
"Author! Author!"

Calvin and Julie Draw
Kevin Rabas

"What do you miss most about home?" Julie said.

"Drumming at Costello's Greenhouse," Calvin said. "There was a little jam session there, nights, in that fine Italian restaurant, with the band set up under the arch of the window where the plants used to be. The drummer Tommy Ruskin hosted, and the old folks all came out to listen. They ordered martinis, and they swizzled their olives in their cups with their liver spotted hands and clapped for every act. Mackey would limp up the three steps to the stage, collapsible cane in hand, and when he sat down it would vanish, like in a magic trick, and he'd have a batch of silk flowers in his hand. Of course, he always sang 'Mack the Knife.'"

"Of course."

"One night Cecil cut his hand on his slide trombone, and he pulled his blue kerchief from his suit coat pocket and dabbed at the blood. He was fine. But the production brought an 'ahh' and 'ohh' from the crowd. He kept playing, unharmed.

"Tommy taught me how to solo. How to tell a story across the drums. I miss him dearly. He'd give me one or two more tunes than the others, tunes that led to gigs. He was like an artistic father to me."

"Draw me one of those solos," Julie said. "Draw me your drums. Draw me one of those nights."

And Calvin did. He put waves and half circles in the air above the drums, music like colors in the air. He put notes, strings of triplets and runs of fast sixteenth notes. He put blue notes. He put whole notes. He put rolls and quick rests. He drew the drum set as if it were a series of circles and half-circles, cymbals and drums.

"I'm pre-art therapy," Julie said. "It helps, art therapy, you know. It helps me. It helps you. It helps a lot of people."

"Sketch for me your schizophrenia," Calvin joked.

"And you can do that, too."

Princess Buttercup
Mike Graves

"I love you."

"I love you back."

Bea lay on an overstuffed pillow, her arms tossed above her head. Long curls framed her flushed, smiling face.

"I need chocolate."

"Chocolate?"

"Chocolate."

"What happens if the princess doesn't get chocolate?"

"She turns into the Wicked Witch of the West. She flies through the sky on a broom and cackles and screeches and commands her troop of winged monkeys to destroy all that was once kind and good."

"Oh, wow. And if she gets her chocolate?"

"She remains the beautiful princess Buttercup, loved and desired by all, but forever faithful and devoted to only one, her handsome and brave hero, Westley."

Miles reached for the phone.

"As you wish."

Thirty minutes later room service had delivered a crystal bowl of chocolate mousse, a mocha fudge brownie, and a pair of dark chocolate and almond truffles. They sat crossed legged on the bed munching on sweets and sipping dark roast coffee. Miles scooped a spoonful of mousse and fed it to Bea.

"This was a great idea, princess."

"Stick with me, kiddo. You can't go wrong."

Miles nibbled on a truffle.

"I believe I will."

They exchanged coffee and chocolate flavored kisses. They sat in bed and talked. Miles told Bea about his hopes for tenure, and Bea told Miles about her dream of becoming a published writer. They talked about growing up. As a young girl, Bea loved being with her dad doing "guy" things. She loved to go fishing and sleep in a tent and stare into a crackling campfire. Miles grew up with what he referred to as the three B's – baseball, books, and his bicycle.

"Now I can add a fourth B to that list."

Bea leaned over and kissed him on the cheek.

"You didn't ride a green bicycle, did you?"

"No, mine was red with big balloon tires and a bell on the handlebars. It was a Schwinn, though."

"Close enough."

"As you wish."

Princess Buttercup fell into Westley's arms, and the handsome hero held the princess and kissed her and loved her as the capital city's winter lights sparkled outside the window.

***

They spent another three days in Washington, D.C., trying to see everything, knowing it was impossible. Each morning they mounted an attack on the National Mall. They went to the National Archives and stood before the Declaration of Independence. Miles was saddened by the decay it had suffered in the past decades. He recalled being moved by its words as an eleven-year-old boy reading it under glass, but those words had faded in the ensuing years. Curators had been forced to move it out of the light, and the words on the dull parchment were barely visible.

They visited the National Air and Space Museum. Bea was taken by the space vehicles, the Friendship 7 and Apollo 11.

"Look at how small they are. I'd never be able to squeeze into that."

Miles was taken by the older aircraft, especially the Spirit of St. Louis.

"Imagine crossing the Atlantic in that thing, navigating by the stars."

During the next few days, they visited the Capitol Building, and the Library of Congress, and art museums, and they strolled through the city. They tried Greek food and Italian food, and they bought sandwiches at neighborhood delis to eat in their room at night. On their last day, they walked down Connecticut Avenue and passed a jewelry store. Miles smiled to himself as he recalled those cheap bracelets he'd bought for his sixth-grade girlfriend. He took Bea by the arm.

"Let's stop here."

Bea looked up at the sign over the door that read "Tiny Jewel Box."

"What for?"

"Come on. I need to do this."

They went inside.

"I'd like to buy something for you, Bea. Do you mind?"

"Miles, that's not necessary. This trip is costing you so much."

Miles was already looking in the display case. He had an idea. He passed by the rings and necklaces and watches. Miles was a sucker for tradition. The shopkeeper came over.

"May I help you?"

"I'd like to see your bracelets."

The clerk led them to the bracelet display. Most were gold and featured diamonds or other precious stones.

"Do you have anything in turquoise and silver?"

The clerk pointed out a silver bracelet with a large triangular stone that was almost heart shaped.

"Do you like this one, Bea?"

Bea looked at the bracelet and then at Miles.

"It's beautiful."

"Good. I'll take it."

Bea put on the bracelet and smiled. She hugged Miles.

"Thank you, sweetheart. Every time I look at it, I'll think of this trip together."

They went back to their room early that afternoon. There was much left to see and do, but the rest of the city would have to wait. They decided to spend their final evening alone in their room, away from tourists and crowds and exhibits. They snuggled in bed, ordered a room service meal, and tried not to think about home and responsibilities.

"Thank you, Miles. Thank you for this adventure."

"I hope we have many more."

The flight from Washington, D.C. arrived in Kansas City early in the afternoon. Bea had planned on staying in Kansas City to spend Christmas with her family. Miles would go on to Wichita to see his folks.

"I want you to meet them, Miles."

"Okay, but I don't want to seem rude. Tell them I can only stay for a few minutes. I want to get to Wichita this evening."

Bea called her folks but got their message machine instead.

"Do you believe my parents? Neither of them has a cell phone. They must be the only people in this hemisphere who still use a land line."

"Not so fast, Bea. My parents don't use cell phones either."

"You must be kidding."

Miles drove south from the airport on Highway 29 and picked up 635 toward Shawnee Mission. The mid-afternoon traffic moved along swiftly, and thankfully they had little construction to battle. They stopped in front of Bea's house on Mastin Street.

"It looks pretty quiet."

Bea used her key to unlock the door, and a quick search found the house empty.

"Bummer. I wanted my parents to meet you."

"I'll meet them, Bea. Next time."

They stood in the living room and hugged and kissed.

"I had a great time, Miles."

"Me, too. I love you."

"I love you back."

"Miss me?"

"I do already."

"Merry Christmas."

"Merry Christmas."

Miles left. He drove south on 35 and picked up the turnpike at Emporia. Along the way he thought about the trip to D.C., his love for Bea, their time together. He thought about the future. He thought he couldn't be happier. They'd be apart for the remainder of the holidays, but they'd be together again after the New Year. Miles turned on the radio. He felt good. He needed some tunes.

He didn't hear his cell phone ring, but its flashing light caught his eye. Bea's name came up on the ID.

"Oh, Miles, did you hear the news?"

"What news? I've been driving. I just turned the radio on a few minutes ago."

"Two of our students died, Miles, a man and a woman. There was a fire in their apartment. No one could get to them in time. It's so horrible."

Bea was crying.

"Who were they?"

Bea gave him the details. The couple had shared an apartment near campus. She had known the woman. They'd taken an art class together a year ago. The young man had been a student in a composition class Miles taught several semesters ago. Miles recalled him as being serious about his schoolwork but always happy and smiling. They still greeted each other in passing on campus. At least they had. Bea talked some more about how unfair life is. She hung up, and Miles turned off the radio. He drove the rest of the way to Wichita in silence.

Tattoo
Kevin Rabas

Julie and Calvin were people watching in Aggieville, seated on metal chairs on patio of the coffee shop, when three guys in their 20s walked by, all with tattoos on arms and legs, Chinese words on latino men.

"He's got his socks pulled up high, stylin'," Julie said. "It's in again."

"That or he's hiding his ankle tattoo, the one that says soy sauce," Calvin said.

Julie said she had a Chinese character tattoo.

"Look." She pulled the back of her shirt up, and Calvin spotted the top of her pink g-string. He didn't look too long.

"What's it say?" Calvin said.

"Optimism. And I checked with my Chinese friends to make sure it was right."

"Smart thinking," Calvin said. "Plus, so many people misspell optimism."

"How?"

"The second vowel, O for I."

Calvin thought she doesn't seem to mind too much that I looked, that she showed me, but for two beats she seems to think back at what might have just started. Calvin goes back in his mind and imagines tracing the Chinese character with his finger. What would she do?

"Can I see it again?" Calvin asked, and he traced the lines with his finger. She turned and kissed him.

Worst Date

Mike Graves

"What's the worst date you've ever been on?"

"Oh, no, here we go."

"It's tough to pick just one."

"It's been so long since I've been on a date."

"That's because you're married, and you're old."

"Stuff it, Miles."

"Yeah, Miles, fess up. You're the one who isn't married. Tell us about a date that was a real nightmare."

Miles swiveled on the bar stool and tipped his bottle of beer. He smiled at his brothers and shook his head.

"Okay guys. There was one date. It was back in high school. The girl was Brenda Van Allen."

"I remember Brenda. She was cute. How could a date with her be a nightmare?"

"Well, it had nothing to do with Brenda, really. It was me. I hadn't dated much. I was a nerd, a real klutz."

"Yeah, I remember."

"Hey, quiet. This is Miles's story. Go ahead, Miles"

Miles put the bottle down on the bar and cleared his throat. He gathered his thoughts and began the story of the worst date he'd ever had.

"Brenda, your date is here."

I heard the woman's voice on the other side of the door as I shifted back and forth on the porch. I looked at my reflection in the glass storm door and straightened my tie and smoothed my hair. I was greeted by a smiling woman wearing a faded housedress and gray tennis shoes with holes worn over her little toes. She looped a strand of hair around an ear.

"I'm Brenda's mother. Come in."

I introduced myself and entered a family room. A heavy man holding a can of Budweiser watched a portable TV.

"Brenda will be right down. Have a seat with Harold. Brenda, your date is here!"

"How do you do, Mr. Van Allen?"

Brenda's dad reminded me of a bear, his forearms matted with dark hair. Black eyes peered from beneath a heavy brow.

"I understand you're taking my daughter to a dance tonight."

"Yes, sir, that's right. Actually, we're going to dinner first, then to a dance at the school."

"You an athlete?"

"Yes, sir. I play centerfield."

Van Allen nodded and pulled on his beer.

"One rule. You gotta get Brenda home by midnight. No later. She goes to church in the morning. Understand?"

"Yes, sir."

Brenda came to the rescue.

"Goodnight, Daddy."

She leaned over to peck his cheek, then took my arm, and hustled me out the door.

"Sorry about that. Daddy can be a little scary at times, but don't let him get to you. He's a pussycat."

"Yea, right."

Dinner went well until the waitress asked if we'd like more tea. I lifted my glass and my fingers slipped. The glass crashed to the table. Tea and ice exploded onto Brenda's pale yellow blouse.

"I'm sorry!"

The waitress and Brenda both dabbed at the tea stains.

I paid the bill, and we left. I apologized again, but we drove in silence. I reached to turn on the radio and noticed what looked like a piece of lint on Brenda's knee. I wanted to be helpful. I picked it off, and when I did her nylons split apart like a ripe melon. I stared at the run that traveled from above her knee to her toes.

"What did you just do?!"

"I saw this piece of lint, and I just wanted to help."

I was really embarrassed.

"Would you like to go back home and change?"

"No, keep going, we're almost there now."

Tea stained her blouse. She had a run in her stocking. I was ready to call it quits, but we pressed on. At the school, Brenda dashed to the ladies room. She was gone forever. I felt like a leper.

She came back, and the dance went pretty well. I was a klutz with no sense of rhythm, but I pretended I was cool. I stepped on Brenda's feet, but it was nice to be holding someone soft and warm.

My best friend, Greg, sauntered over with his date, Nan. Greg drove a Chevy convertible.

"Let's go for a ride."

We left the dance and jumped into the convertible. Brenda and I snuggled in the back seat. I forgot about the spilled tea, the ruined nylons, and stepping on Brenda's toes. I raised my arm to draw Brenda close to me.

"Ouch!"

Greg and Nan turned around.

"What happened?"

I couldn't speak. I stared. My elbow had cracked Brenda's nose.

"I'm bleeding!"

Indeed, she was. Red drops dribbled down her chin and fell onto the yellow blouse. Tea stains were no longer an issue.

"I'm sorry. I'm sorry."

I wiped Brenda's chin with a tissue. She pushed my hand away. She sat in the corner with her head tilted back and her forearm across her eyes. Greg turned onto a dirt road that ended in a blueberry field. I felt terrible. Nan screamed.

"Look out!"

The car bumped to a halt.

"What happened?"

We were buried up to our axles in mud.

"What are we going to do?"

I glanced at my watch – 11:30. Greg opened the door.

"There was a farm house about a mile back."

He stepped out of the car and sank to his shins.

"Son of a bitch."

I looked at the soup surrounding the car and realized I couldn't jump to dry ground. I stepped into the mud. We slopped and slogged to higher ground and began walking. After a mile or so we came to a farm house. The house was dark.

"I think we're going to get a farmer out of bed."

"We have no choice."

It's hard to tell which woke the farmer, the doorbell or the barking dog. Either way, he was fuming as he listened to our story.

"What the hell were you doing on that road?

"Could you please pull us out, mister?"

We looked at the John Deere tractor parked alongside the barn.

"We'll pay you."

He grumbled and swore, but he moved toward the John Deere. It took a while to pull out the car, but we were grateful. We reached for our wallets. We had five dollars between us. The farmer looked at each of us. He shook his head and snatched the money.

I looked at my watch. It was 1:00 AM. We were a mess. An hour later I turned into Brenda's driveway.

"If the door is unlocked, I can sneak in."

We climbed the steps and tried the door. It was unlocked. Finally, we had a stroke of luck. We were two hours late. I was covered in mud. Brenda was covered in blood. Nothing had gone well the entire evening. Still, it was a beautiful evening. We stood on the porch holding hands in the moonlight.

"I'm sorry things went so badly. I hope you won't be angry with me."

I drew Brenda closer and bent to kiss her. The porch light flashed on, and the door flew open. The bear towered over me. He wore rumpled pajamas. His black eyes blazed. A trickle of saliva ran down his chin. He roared.

"Young man, would you please stop leaning on the doorbell!"

No Sex
Kevin Rabas

Calvin took Julie back to his part of the yellow house, its paint flaked and crumbled; it came off in fly-paper yellow strips in the wind. Julie took her top off and said, "Let's touch, but no sex, not until I'm married."

"I hadn't thought of that," Calvin said.

"So think of it," Julie said and twirled a silver cross held on a black string around her neck.

"Besides," she said, "I'm moving into Chaucer House next week, which is all girls, all Christian, and we can't do it there."

This was ok with Calvin. He loved Julie and wanted her, but he could wait, it could wait. Julie threw her shirt at his face.

Jazz Combo 2, Performance Number One
Kevin Rabas

The house lights dimmed to black, and Calvin and the band were bathed in white light, while the audience sank into darkness, unseeable, gone, disappeared into red seat cushions and into the near silence of mumblings and peppermint star-candy wrapper twisting and unfurling. One mint for the show, someone's grandmother thought.

Jazz Combo 2 played Friday night, with Calvin on drums. Calvin raised his sticks, ready for the conductor's hand to drop. The first few notes were important; hit with conviction because what you set up continued, and so many people judge by what they first hear, first see. We will all hit, blow, strum, and ivory plunk together. Calvin thought: ONE, and they all did.

Calvin played with heart and passion, when he soloed, his hands and arms circling the drums in triangles and squares and circles, swarming and swirling and spinning, the drum tips and sticks blurred. He played quiet, sparse passages, then medium hits, moans in response. He double, then single-stroke rolled on the low tom, an elephant's moan, a thunderstorm, a herd of wildebeests stampeding. He told the story of his own calling out into the night for Bea, the washing machine spun, then stopped, with his clothes inside. He played that. He played the silences and the solemn, caring notes of his talk with Julie about her Dad, the phone line between them, the curlicues of the phone cord, the metal lines stretched between crucifix wooden poles, carrying the voices across the miles, from small college town to suburb to city, Kansas City. The recent memories made their way into song, across the drum, and the last story Calvin played was a story still unfolding, still coming, a love story, a call for Julie to join him, to dance with him across the stage, a slow dance, a quiet dance, a dance cheek to cheek.

When the solo ended, the concert was over. They were last. Julie came up onto stage beaming, like a groupie, like an undiscovered lover, like a fan. Calvin hugged her, and showed the others he knew her, and loved her, and was hers, and they patted him on the back or threw two fingers up at him, and said things like, "Nice solo, Cal," and "We're gonna have to throw some water on those drums next time. You were smokin', man." Calvin played better in performance, under pressure, when the lights shined hottest. He rose to the moment. He loved that about the body, about his own way, and he did not neglect it or take it for granted. He practiced and rehearsed towards it, towards stamina and heart, skill and will.

Julie took a cymbal stand in hand, and said, "What do I do with this?" and Calvin showed her how to break it down, how to spin the lug nut to let the cymbal off and how to take the legs and fold them in. Together, they broke the set down and hauled it across the parking lot that had its first light glaze of ice of the season, white and light blue on black. Calvin felt honored to have a woman with him who would help, who would think to help him carry his cymbals and drums across the iced parking lot, like a fan, like an enamored woman on a first date. It was like starting all over again. He was in love, and he wanted to play for her every night, woo her, pour his heart across the drums like lightning bugs or fire. He kissed her when they got to the car door and to the trunk. And she did not put her bag down at once, but kissed and kissed, and only when he drew her closer did she let her arm lower and set the drum bag on the ground, and her left foot went up.

Calvin on Jazz
Kevin Rabas

Julie asked, "Why did you close your eyes when you played that long solo?"

"I didn't think about it much. I just do," Calvin said. "You know, jazz musicians close their eyes because what they do is like having sex in front of other people. And the musicians don't always want to see—and be influenced—by the audience's reactions, by what you say and do, how you react."

"Really? That's kind of sexy, Calvin. I always found jazz music insular before. There's a guy up there with a soprano sax, and he's noodling around to himself, holding long, crooning low notes, then whispering, calling, then soloing in a long flurry of notes only he knows or hears or understands. It seemed so masturbatory. But here you are saying the musicians are getting it on with each other, and they're not so sure they want us all to watch."

"Yes. I think you have it there. And sometimes, too, they're playing right to you in the front row, playing their heart out to you, not Kenny G with his blonde locks and his long, low notes, but a man from the streets whose notes are all earned, whose voice and whose moves are genuine, earned and new. He's doing something no one else has done before in exactly that same way. And his heart is coming out of his horn."

"That's beautiful. Will you draw it for me?"

"Sure," said Calvin. Julie brought out the paper and the pencils, and he did.

Dark Thoughts

Mike Graves

Miles lay in a bed in his parent's house in Wichita. Everyone had gone to bed. Miles had been reading a novel by Richard Russo. Now he closed the book and turned out the light. He put his hands behind his head and stared at the darkness. He listened to the quiet. He thought about the past several days, weeks. Where had his life been a few months ago? Where was his life now? A trip to the nation's capital. A flight that soared close to the moon. Hungry passion distanced from reality. Romance sped quickly. Too quickly? A vague memory, a kernel of thought, stirred in his mind, remaining shapeless, out of reach. Go slowly.

Miles rolled over onto his side. He thought of Bea and wondered if she were thinking of him. He hoped she was. He hoped her thoughts were happy thoughts and her night was peaceful. He closed his eyes and slept.

Miles couldn't know Bea was thinking of him, of them. Miles couldn't know Bea was being seduced by the pulse of the music, the rhythms taking her away. She swayed and let herself be carried. She rode the drift, rising and lowering with the song, always the song. How she missed the music. She listened to the beat, the heart pounding notes running hot and cold and felt the fever and the chill. She closed her eyes and traveled to another place, swaying, swaying. Her fingers probed the bracelet on her wrist.

Miles couldn't know this. He couldn't see her sitting in the jazz club, couldn't hear the sounds. He couldn't see Bea's sister lean across the table. He couldn't hear her sister ask above the music.

"Bea? Bea? Where are you, Bea?"

Calvin Runs, Plans
Kevin Rabas

Calvin, his running shorts on, his keys on a loop around his neck, jingling, ran laps around the oval track that overlooked the weights machines in the K-State rec center. While he ran, he watched the clock. Eight minute mile. Seven forty-five. Seven fifty. He wasn't too bad. Halfway through, he concentrated on his breath. Breathe in, breathe in, breathe it all out. Calvin had a touch of asthma, and swimming had taught him how to breathe, how to breathe out hard through a crack at the edge of his lips. Get that bad air out, so you can breathe in strong, fill the lungs for the next set of breaths. In the water, a string of bubbles would jet out of that hole at the edge of the lips, quick and lithe, like a school of small fish darting all together.

Calvin tried to run 2-3 times a week to keep a bit of endurance up. As he ran what he thought might be his final three laps, eight laps equaled a mile, Slim Sally jogged up to him and caught his pace, said, "Hey, Cal. You entering the Flint Hills Poetry Society Contest?"

"Sure," Cal said. "Planning on it."

These were Slim Sally's first laps of the day. Each footfall, each breath was easy for her. She glided over the blue rubber surface of the track. She didn't even seem to touch down. Her feet just wisped past the surface. She was lithe; she was quick. Her breath came easy, and she could smile as she ran, her teeth white, her lips cocked open with that smile of the '30s, young Katharine Hepburn's mock grin.

"Whatcha gonna send?" Sally said.

"I have this theory," Calvin said. "Holden likes things with zest, sexy poems. I'm going to send him 'Indiscretion' and a few others like that. He's a man who loves life and appreciates love and lust. Rabelaisian. That's my first take. That's what I think."

"I have some love poems," Slim Sally said.

"Good," Calvin said. "Send them."

Calvin wanted so badly to be found, to be recognized, to make a start, a go. To be a writer, you had to get some hits. You had to win sometimes. You had to publish. Calvin was just starting, and it was important to him to get on the board. Slim Sally knew this too and thought the same. Calvin and Sally ran a few more laps. Calvin completed one last mile, and then Sally put out her slim, bony hand, and said, "Shake. Good luck to you."

"Good luck to us both. I think we might win."
"Can't win, if we don't send," Slim Sally said.

Calvin Writes Toward the Contest
Kevin Rabas

Calvin sat at his Apple Quadra 640, a tan box with a Little Mermaid screen saver, which his techie neighbor put on the console as a joke. The cartoon fish-girl swam, her red hair water-blown, until the sharks came. Then she zipped away, and behind her on the ocean floor that singing crab friend of hers scuttled across wet sand, his ragged claws raised.

Calvin thought of Julie. He'd write a love poem, the hardest kind. He needed a few more works for the Flint Hills Poetry Society Contest. He'd tap out the draft for a new one this afternoon, if he could. He opened the dusty, bent, yellow-white venetian blinds to full and let the afternoon light in. Dust motes billowed by the blinds. They made paths in the air and swarmed when he moved his hands through them. We're all in entropy, Calvin thought. One moves, and it all moves. One changes, and the whole community, whole cloud might change, too.

Calvin wrote this:

When you told me your father had almost died,

his heart now a week heart, a small heart

in a big man, you put your hand on my hand,

and we steered your car together. We shifted

together, and drove to the water.

At the water's edge, I taught you

how to skip rocks, how the strong light touch

makes the rock hop across water

without sinking, how life can be light

if we let it. We don't have to sink,

like a rock, like a broken heart, like a body

too full, held too long without

that lightness, without enough love

to skip, to sail, to rise in an arc, and fall.

Calvin knew that draft was too easy, too light. He'd try again later. He printed the poem and signed it, and wrote a quick note to Julie to go with it. He'd give it to Julie tomorrow. A quick love letter. This reminded Calvin of Tamara, a girl he dated in high school. She was two years younger than him, the age of his sister, and his sister and Tamara were friends. Both Alice, his sister, and Tamara were on student council and were well liked at school. Calvin loved Tamara, and he wrote her a poem a day, which she kept in a yellow notebook. He loved that she kept them, that she read them, that she pretended to understand.

Zebras & Flags
Mike Graves

"Oh, no! A flag! A flag!"

"What? Not against Kansas City!"

"What's the call?"

The TV announcer went silent and waited for the referee on the field to turn on his mic and make the call. The ref made a chopping signal at the back of his knee.

"Clipping, Kansas City, number 62. Fifteen yard penalty from the point of infraction. Third down."

"Oh, man."

"Just when the Chiefs were starting to move the ball."

"The zebras ruin this game."

Miles shook his head and reached for the bowl of popcorn. He loved his brothers and his dad and enjoyed being with them. That included watching TV. He just had trouble connecting with pro sports teams. He couldn't feel emotion for a bunch of spoiled prima donnas who play a game and earn seven figure salaries doing it. It all seemed absurd.

"Pass the popcorn, Miles."

Miles stood up and handed the popcorn to his dad. He used it as an excuse to leave the room. Outside on the porch, Miles sat on the rail and embraced the cold. It made him come alive. He inhaled deeply and watched his foggy breath drift away. His thoughts turned to Bea. He wondered what she was doing at this moment. He looked down the block and noticed a group of children sledding on a small hill. He reached into his pocket for his phone and held it in his palm. He stared at the dial pad. He and Bea had agreed to spend time with their families and not contact each other. They agreed it was best to not dwell on their relationship over the holidays.

"We'll enjoy the holidays apart. It will be good for us. We'll get back together after the New Year."

Actually, it had been Bea's idea, but Miles had agreed. It made sense. Neither of them would enjoy being with their families if all they did was think about each other. The plan had sounded good a week ago, but now Miles wasn't so sure. It was the day after Christmas, meaning New Year's Day was almost another week away. Miles didn't want to wait another week to see Bea. He wondered if she was thinking the same thing.

He looked at the phone again. Across the street, a couple of high school kids yelled and threw snow balls at each other. One got clobbered in the ear and screamed a profanity. The other laughed and ran.

Miles dialed her number. The phone rang. It rang again and again. Miles had decided he wouldn't leave a message. She'd see that he'd called. That would be enough. He gave up on the fourth ring and started to hang up when the ringing stopped. First he heard a click, then music, jazz he thought. After a beat, a too long beat, he heard her voice.

"Hello, Miles."

Miles stamped his feet on the porch and pulled his collar around his neck. His frosty breath floated in front of his face.

"Hi, Bea… how are you?"

The horn faded and a sax picked up the thread. Brushes swished on the drums.

"I'm fine."

"I miss you, Bea. I needed to hear your voice."

The sax wailed.

"I thought we agreed we wouldn't contact each other until after the holidays."

Miles stamped his feet again. He felt light-headed and cold.

"Yeah, Bea, I know, I know, but I miss you. What have you been up to?"

"Miles, I'll talk to you next week, okay?"

"Okay, fine. We'll talk next week. Do you love me, Bea?"

A trombone jumped in, and the drummer went back to sticks.

"Miles, please don't do this. Yes, I love you. I do. But I need to go slowly. I told you that right at the beginning. I need to slow down. Please don't be clingy, Miles."

Miles closed his eyes.

"Merry Christmas, Bea."

"Merry Christmas, Miles. I'll talk to you next week."

"Yeah. Next week."

Miles clicked off his phone and stared into the distance. Children walked in the snowy street pulling a sled behind them. Teenage boys ran between houses throwing snowballs at each other. Roars from his brothers and dad in the den carried to the porch. The Chiefs must have scored a touchdown. Somewhere far away Bea listened to jazz. Miles felt cold. He stood for a moment longer and then went back into the house.

Bea and All That Jazz
Kevin Rabas

Bea had always said she wanted a bass player. Calvin figured eventually she'd get herself one. But for now, he thought, she'd settle for a drummer; that's what he thought months ago. It was a small surprise, but still a surprise when Calvin found a program from the university jazz concert in his mailbox, hand delivered, with a message from Bea written on it: "Good show, tonight, Slinger! I've missed your music. I never liked jazz until I met you. How are you? Call me, dear friend." Calvin wasn't sure what to do. Easily he could screw up what he had with Julie by calling Bea. Julie hated Bea, and Bea hated Julie. Calvin kept remembering how Bea once said, "You'll leave me for someone I hate, like that little hot Julie, one day." Bea had been flirting with another GTA, and Slim Sally danced up to him, and said, "She's going to leave with him. You'd better get in there, Sport. If it doesn't work out, Cal, know you can always leave with me." Some said Sally was too much, but Calvin always saw her as honest. Scheming, but honest. He didn't mind all that. Bea didn't leave with Biff. She left with Calvin, but that night Calvin called her on it, and that's when she said that bit about Julie. Bea was right. Julie came right over when Bea was done with him.

Calvin got his brushes out. He turned on a video of Calhoun playing brushes, doing tricks like the "salad mixer" and showing ways, also, to play lots of circular strokes when playing slow, ways to fill the bar, but with subtlety, with grace, with lots and lots of long, sustained swish. He didn't know what to do. He played for hours, swishing slow, until he fell asleep with the wire brushes in his hands.

Black & Decker
Kevin Rabas

Calvin thought of a story from his past, before he started having sex. He'd returned to that time with Julie. She wanted them to—and they would—wait. He thought about that innocent time when he was living at home, before he graduated, before he came to K-State. He thought he might write it out as a story, and he did:

Black & Decker

The white lights of the movie credits were the only thing that illuminated the room, and Calvin's hand was too close to Maxine's hand, but they did not touch. Maxine gave Calvin a solemn, serious look, then flashed a smile—and her braces glinted silver in the movie light. It was a first date. Maxine played third trumpet in Jazz Band 2, and Calvin played drums. Maxine had a wild streak, and Calvin took to it. "You know what you call a black girl with braces who gives you a blow job?" Maxine said. Calvin had no idea. "Black and Decker pecker wrecker," she said—and her braces caught light, and Calvin kissed her to stop her laughter. He noticed glitter around her eyes. "You're so glittery," he said, "I try," she said, and pulled him closer—and they hugged, and Calvin put his hand on her lower back, which was smooth and warm— and his hand touched the top of her thong, and stopped, and he thought: Where will the night go next? Calvin is 21, and Maxine 23—they live in KC, the city of fountains. Maxine said she wants to teach music, and Calvin's taking the class just to keep his chops up, to be able to gig while he works at the school paper and the music library, and studies jazz. His music friends call him Scoop; he always has his reporter's notebook, and he writes down rhythms and chord changes in Big Band 2. Maxine watches him, wonders what he's up to. She only pencils in a few accents, glosses a few notes, in pencil, on her chart, and she leaves the rest to guess and to chance and to the drone of the horn section to cover up. "Think we should've gone to the party?" Maxine said, and Calvin answers, "Never." There was a band party after tonight's show at Brad's place a few doors down, and Calvin told his mother, whom he still lives with, that that was where he'd be. He lied. Maxine and he ditched. They chose a movie, The Body Guard, and went their own way, settled into the couch together, bet on love over sound, over music, over Big Band Jazz. Calvin's mother says she hates Maxine, says she looks evil up there on the top row, her trumpet up, golden, catching white stage light, her lips smirked, her top low, her abundance of pale midriff. Calvin likes that, but he doesn't know about Maxine, but he did like her kiss, that first taste, like brandy and rainbow sugar sprinkles. She must drink. She must drink a lot. Maxine says she wants Calvin to stay the night, and Calvin considers. He touches Maxine's back again, that warm open spot, like a valley in the dunes, sun-kissed. He notices about 10 belts draped over the radiator, men's belts. Maxine says those are from her roommate's men; they leave them when they go, forgetting. "Slut," she says, and laughs. Calvin doesn't want it to begin and end like this; he's not so sure about Maxine. He wants her, but he doesn't know how bad or how long. "How about we get dinner tomorrow," he says, "then hit the jams together in the night?" "Ok," she says, "but don't think I'm loose," and she gives that smirk Calvin's mother hates, and Calvin kisses her, long and slow, like in Woody Allen kisses, and she shuts the door, and Calvin goes to his car, his blue and white Blazer, and he realizes his keys are there still in the ignition, locked inside, and he's 15 highway minutes from home— and he can't stay. His mother would notice, and ma is the only one he can now call to get home.

Calvin Writes Toward the Contest 2
Kevin Rabas

When Calvin woke up, his brushes were in hand. He put them down and picked up a pad of paper and pen and stretched the paper across the snare drum head, the lined paper over the dirty white cow skin head, the face of the head marked silver and black, smudged by drum stick and brush swipe. He wrote towards the contest. 3 am, and he thought: What if this were my last hour, my last chance? What would I do with my life. He thought about what he had left to do tonight, and he wrote the poem. Then he did what it said.

When You Begin

Calvin gave himself half an hour

to write like it was the end,

his last 30 minutes up top, above,

in sun, on dirt, alive with breath and pen-scratch.

But he only wrote two anecdotes

and part of a letter and a comment/critique

to a new student. The letter

was to his sister.

This is how it is. We do

what we always do, even

in the end. So we must train

ourselves to do last things, true

things, bright things with each breath.

Any small moment just might be it, the end.

Begin with that, when you begin.

Once done, Calvin put the letter to his sister into the box out front. Then he took another look at Bea's note. When the sun came up, he thought he might walk over to her apartment, see if she was there.

What Do Women Want?

Mike Graves

"What do women want?"

Miles tossed the question into the room.

His brothers and his dad looked at each other, then at Miles. Someone snickered, someone choked, and finally everyone began to laugh. Everyone but Miles, of course. The laughter drew the women into the room, his mother and his brother's wives. His dad pointed the remote at the TV and turned down the volume.

"Miles wants to know what women want. Where did that question come from, Miles?"

His brother, Randy, shook his head.

"I don't know, Miles. For a professor, you sure can be dense. Who knows what women want? Women don't know what they want."

His mother disagreed.

"That's not fair. Women aren't that mysterious. Men just don't pay attention."

The football game was over. The Chiefs had eked out a victory at home, and now the talking heads were showing replays and arguing calls in the tedious post game analysis. Miles was pleased his dad had muted the sound. His other brother, Don, chimed in.

"I pay attention, Mom. I know what my wife wants."

Everyone turned to Don.

"Enlighten us."

"It's easy. Cindy wants me to want whatever she wants."

There were a few groans. Cindy smiled.

"That answer's a cop out."

"No it isn't. Look, sometimes Cindy wants to go shopping and she wants me to go along. Now she knows I hate to go shopping, but she wants me to go anyway. But here's the kicker. I can't please her by just tagging along. There's more to it than that. To please Cindy, I have to want to go, even when I don't want to go."

Randy shook his head.

"Give me a break."

Cindy gave her husband a hug and spoke.

"It's true. A woman doesn't just want roses from her man. A woman wants her man to want to give her roses. It makes all the difference in the world."

Miles had another question.

"So what does a woman want when she doesn't want something?"

His mother put her hand on his knee.

"What's troubling you, Miles?"

Miles went silent, and someone else spoke.

"Obviously it's a woman."

"Yeah, spill Miles."

"What's up?"

Miles asked the question, knowing the answer, dreading to hear it spoken.

"What does a woman mean when she says she wants to go slowly? What does it mean when she says you are being too clingy?"

There was a brief pause before Don spoke.

"That's easy. The woman is in love with someone else."

Miles didn't respond, but others did.

"Hey, that's not fair. Maybe she just wants some space."

"Yeah, right. Space to share with another guy."

"Not necessarily. Love takes time."

"There's another guy."

Miles heard the comments without listening. He knew the answers to his questions. The trip to D.C., the hand holding on the Great Mall, the intimate dinners, the lovemaking in the hotel, had all been a dream. The dream had been meaningful, but it meant more to Miles than to Bea. Miles loved Bea. Bea did not love Miles, at least not in the same way. Was Bea capable of love, of loving just one man? Did Bea even want love? Maybe she wanted to be alone. Miles could respect that, even if it hurt. These questions roiled in his mind, but there was one other question that was more difficult to address. Miles knew the question and feared the answer. Was Bea in love with someone else?

Bea, Thunder, Tub

Kevin Rabas

Dark thunderhead clouds rolled over campus, and it started to pour grey drops, bucketfuls. Storms could come and go, like a line of Mack trucks, unexpectedly in Kansas, especially to those who didn't watch the weather, and Calvin didn't anymore. With his parents he did. His parents were sons and daughters of Kansas farmers, up at 5 am.

Calvin was halfway to Bea's when it started coming down, and he ran, his body, his clothes, bone drenched. He shivered, then he shook. His teeth chattered. He ran, full out, through puddles, through mud, through grass turning to slop, to runnels and rivulets and swamps of water, the water rising halfway to the tops of the grass blades, then running over them like in-land streams, on-campus streams—a deluge was upon little Manhattan.

People stopped driving. People hurried home. All of the sudden all the windows burned yellow and blue. People sat at home, hunkered in. The blue glow of their TVs filling their rooms, they waited for it to stop.

Calvin arrived at Bea's door. He rang. He knocked.

She laughed when she opened up.

"You look like a drowned rat."

"Can I come in?" he said.

"Yes, yes," she laughed. "Come in. I'll get you a towel. Stand right there on the mat." She gave him the towel. Then her lips curled, and she said, "Don't be shy. Off with it, Cal."

And he peeled off the shirt. It weighed a lot, full of rain. He covered his hips with the towel and walked to the bathroom. The bathtub water was already on, hot. He stepped in. As it filled, he waited for his shivering to stop, his teeth to stop tap-tap-tapping. He concentrated on his body, and did not look up, and so he did not see her until she was beside him, and then in the tub, pressed against his back, warm and pink. Bea was with him in the tub.

She kissed the back of his neck and put her chin on his shoulder.

"This won't be one last time," she said. "I just want to hold you." And the night seemed to dissolve into candles with low wicks, and they slept in the same bed again, held each other, sexless, quiet, like little kids.

Anke Essen, Visiting Poet Reads
Kevin Rabas

Bea went out of town for a girl's night out with her friend Angeline. Calvin went to the poetry reading at the downtown coffee shop. There was a featured reader, followed by an open mic. The featured reader, Anke Essen, with her shoulder-length blonde hair in natural ringlets, talked about American culture, read from her new book *Eagles Black and Bald*, with English on the left hand page and German on the facing page, a book for both continents. Most of the poets in town were there, sitting in grey metal folding chairs, quiet, their mouths open a bit, as if they were tasting the poetry. She read, her slender figure almost disappearing behind the microphone stand:

Jens goes to buy a cellphone at the mall.

His hand pauses over one, a blue X with red

    around it.

"Looks American," he says, and the Indian

man behind the kiosk says, "You may not want that

    one. It's…"

Jens turns over the phone, sees where it

    says "Rebel Flag."

"But I'm a rebel," Jens says, "Was held in

East Germany near the end for assembling."

"It's for rednecks," the Indian man

says. "If I may paraphrase, if I may be blunt."

"American skinheads?"

"Yes," he says. "Yes. That type."

"Schizer," Jens says, and puts a hand

through his long, dark hair. "Fuct."

Calvin didn't know much German, but he got the joke, and watched as a man with a rebel flag hat took it off, ruffled his hair, scratched, and put it back.

When Essen stopped, Calvin went to the john. The lock didn't work, but he had to go. He was up third. There were about two steps between him and the door, he knew, in case someone came in. It was unisex. Almost done, and the door swung open. Calvin stood quick, stopped the door with a hand, but didn't get very well covered up. Essen gasped, but a hand to her slim face, said "Pardon," and left. When Calvin got out, he saw Essen again.

"Very sorry about that," he said.

"My fault entirely." She looked embarrassed, but she smirked.

Calvin sent four poems to her literary magazine, when he got home. He licked the stamp, and thought about his chances. Would embarrassment help or hinder? Couldn't hurt to try.

Bea and Calvin, a Silence
Kevin Rabas

Bea didn't call, and Calvin didn't call either. Their silence was like golden wheat, a wave in the wind, without sound, beautiful to glance at or to watch. Calvin didn't mind if it was over. He wanted her, but he also knew how she was, how she might not settle. He thought about Bea and all her fireworks, all her ability to summon up fire around her, and flash, how she could walk by a storefront window, and the young women and men inside would all watch, would all watch as she marched by. He remembered how she was once invited to the wedding of a young man she once dated, and how the bride hated her. Calvin thought he might write about that, and be done with Bea for a while. If she came by, he would be ok with her, but he wouldn't take up with her again. He was involved with Julie, but love, like love in heaven, was a thing to be shared like children share it. Love was not a thing of jealousy or a thing to be horded. Society kept so many people from each other. He would not help society along. He decided not to mention that last hot bath to Julie. It would probably never come up.

Since he forgot to get his clothes, the ones left in Bea's apartment washer, he married that event with the rainstorm event. That made for a better story.

Red dress,

frog-buttoned in back,

geisha dress

that stopped your rival's wedding,

dress that kept you

from being invited to mine;

red dress,

I forgive, I invite you.

Parade on in.

Hold every curve

as a hand would.

Palm and lift up.

As you pass, know I will remember

that last hot bath you ran me,

when I returned

through the thunderstorm

for the clothes we left

in your apartment's quarter washer,

that afternoon when you told me:

You can stay. We can love.

You can stay. We can love.

When Calvin looked back over the poem Calvin knew Bea would not ask him to stay, and that was ok with him. Life was not always art. Sometimes it was less; sometimes it was more.

A Beer with Calvin

Mike Graves

"You blew it, Miles. You blew it again."

Miles looked around to make sure no one was watching him. He was talking to himself. He did that sometimes. He let his thoughts slip out without thinking. Still, he thought to himself, you did blow it man. You pushed, and Bea resisted. She said to go slowly, you heard her, but you didn't. You've always been like that. You see something you want, and you reach for it. You don't stop to consider the consequences. Now you've done it again. You could have had something beautiful. You did have something beautiful. And you blew it.

Miles walked across the quiet campus, listening to only his thoughts. A north wind whistled through bare tree limbs. He didn't see anyone else. Classes hadn't started back up again. They wouldn't for several days. His folks had asked him to stay in Wichita longer, but he'd resisted. They knew he'd be alone in Manhattan. His brothers and their wives left the day after New Year's, and Miles used that as an excuse to leave, too. He'd come back to Manhattan early. Now he was alone, and his loneliness added to his misery. He'd never learn.

He drifted toward the English building, more out of habit than with purpose. He'd decided earlier he wouldn't go to his office. He'd even left his keys on the dresser so he couldn't change his mind. He was just drifting.

He rounded the corner at the back of the building and stopped. He smiled. There was the bike rack. One lone bike leaned in the rack, the green Schwinn. The bike looked as lonely as he felt. Miles lifted the bike out of the rack. The handlebars felt cold and stiff. Miles turned them back and forth several times to loosen them up. He rang the bell just because he wanted to hear it. He wanted to hear another voice.

"Hello, back at ya."

Miles spoke to the bike and didn't care if anybody heard him. He jumped on and pedaled. He rode around campus, not in a straight line but in a meandering fashion up and down sidewalks, around buildings he rarely entered. He saw a few people, staff probably, and rang the bell and cried out, "Happy New Year!" with a wave.

A north wind blew down his collar, and after several minutes, Miles realized he was cold. He pointed the bike south, off campus, and crossed the street to Starbucks, eager for a hot cup of coffee. Before he reached the door, he could hear B.B. King singing the blues, alerting the world that the thrill is gone.

"Ain't that the truth," Miles pondered.

He reached for the door, and something inside caught his eye. A scarf, a thrift-store scarf. He knew that scarf. He peered through the window, and there she was. Bea. She was sitting on a couch facing into the room. Miles felt a pulse in his temple. He no longer felt cold. Bea wasn't alone on the couch. She was leaning on the shoulder of a young man, a man Miles recognized but couldn't place right away. He recalled the guy was a GTA, but what was his name? Keith? Curtis? Close, but that wasn't right. Kevin? No, no. Calvin. That was it. Calvin. And Bea was leaning against him, and as Miles watched Calvin reached up and put his arm around Bea.

Miles turned around and got back on the bike. He rode away from the coffee shop. He didn't ring the bell. He could hear B.B.'s song fading behind him.

The thrill is gone.

***

"Hello, professor."

"Uh, hello. It's Calvin, isn't it?"

Calvin nodded. Miles and Calvin had passed each other in the hall. Miles was returning to his office, and Calvin had a stack of papers under his arm. Miles checked his watch.

"Say, Calvin, have you got a minute?"

Calvin shrugged.

"Sure, professor. I guess so."

"Call me Miles."

"Okay, Miles."

Miles dropped his books and notes on his desk. He checked his watch again.

"You know, I don't feel like talking here. How about a cup of coffee?"

Calvin shrugged again.

"Sure, okay."

"Better yet, how about a beer?"

"Yeah, better yet."

"You can leave your papers here."

Calvin dropped his papers on the desk, and they left together. It was four o'clock. Miles had planned on grading essays, but the hell with it. As they walked they talked about the new semester's classes. Calvin was teaching Composition I, a requirement for every GTA in the English Department. He wondered what books Miles was covering in his American Novel class, and Miles told him. They crossed the street and cut through Triangle Park. They passed by Rock-a-Belly's. Even at four o'clock the music was too loud for conversation. They turned into Porter's on the next block. Each took a stool at the bar and Miles ordered beer.

"How was your vacation, Calvin?"

Calvin sipped his beer and nodded.

"It was okay. Good, actually."

Miles sipped his beer and nodded.

"Professor... Miles, can I ask you a question?"

"Sure."

"Why are we here? I mean, what's up? We've passed each other in the halls for over a semester. We've always nodded to each other, maybe said hello, but nothing more than that. Now today you invite me for a beer. You ask about my classes and my vacation. Something's on your mind. What's up?"

Miles set his beer on the bar and nodded.

"Fair enough, Calvin. You're right. We've never spoken. That's probably my fault. I have something I'd like to discuss with you, and I don't really know how to begin."

Miles drummed his fingers on the bar. He really did not know how to begin. He started to speak, but something flashed in the corner of his eye.

"Well, look who's here."

He turned on his stool, and Calvin turned with him. Bea looked at both of them and smiled.

"So, what are you boys up to?"

Miles and Calvin said nothing. They stared at Bea. She wore a black beret that listed to the side at just the right angle and a red scarf that contrasted nicely. She wore a black woolen cape that showed some wear and faded jeans tucked into knee-high leather boots slightly scuffed and run-down at the heels. Thrift store purchases that might have made a less confident woman appear unkempt, but on

Bea it worked. She looked stunning.

"What's the matter with you guys? Can't you speak? At least buy a lady a beer."

Miles scooted over one stool, and Bea sat down between them. Miles ordered a round of beers for everyone. He felt awkward and at the same time dazzled by Bea's demeanor. How could she be so cool?

"Okay, I'm going to take a stab in the dark. I'll bet you two were talking about me."

Calvin leaned forward and looked past Bea toward Miles.

"Is this why you brought me here, Miles? Do you know Bea? Were you going to tell me something about Bea?"

Bea furrowed her brow and turned toward Miles.

"Yes, Miles, answer him. Were you going to say something about me?"

Miles looked down at the bar and shook his head.

"Bea, what are you doing here? How did you know we were here?"

"Don't be so paranoid, Miles. I didn't know you were here. I'm meeting Slim Sally for a beer and got here a little early, that's all. I walk in and who should I find but my two darlings, Calvin and Miles. Small world, huh? Or at least a small Aggieville. Stop avoiding the question, Miles. You're wriggling like a six-year-old in church. What were you going to say to Calvin?"

Calvin looked puzzled, but a light was starting to glow. He had to ask.

"Bea, are you and Miles… you know… together?"

Bea shook her head.

"Now Calvin, don't you go paranoid on me, too. We've known each other too long for this."

She rested her fingers on Calvin's arm.

"I'm not with Miles…"

She turned to look at Miles.

"… sorry Miles…," then turned back to Calvin.

"I'm not with anyone. You know me better than that. I've never lied to you, to either of you, and I hope you don't hate me, either of you. I've tried to be honest, and I'm being honest now. We all say we want the people we love to be honest with us, but we don't really mean it. Sometimes honesty hurts. The truth is often painful. That's just the way it is. I'll be honest, but don't ask me to apologize. Don't ask me to become someone I'm not. I won't do that, Calvin, not for you or Miles or anyone. That's the one thing that will drive me away."

Calvin didn't speak. Miles cleared his throat.

"So where do we go from here?"

Bea turned toward Miles.

"Well, Miles darling, I can't speak for you and Calvin, but as for me, I'm moving to that table right over there."

Slim Sally had walked in, and Bea stood up to greet her. They hugged each other and walked to an empty table in the corner. Calvin and Miles sipped their beers and said nothing.

Later, Miles walked around the corner of the building, and the empty bike rack caught his eye. He pulled the coaster out of his pocket and read the address Calvin had written. He recalled Calvin's advice: "Take the bike back."

What struck Miles about meeting Calvin was how much he liked him. Calvin was a likable guy and probably interesting, too. Miles wouldn't mind getting to know him better. Maybe they could discuss music and poetry.

Miles stood by the bike rack and read Bea's address again. He looked off in the distance. Take the bike back. It seemed juvenile at first, but as he thought about it, it seemed like the thing to do. Miles began walking.

It wasn't far, six or seven blocks. He checked the coaster against the number on the building. This was it, and there was the bike. The green Schwinn was tucked behind a shrub, leaning against the wall of the building. Miles pulled the bike out. He sat on it and started to pedal away, but then he stopped. He pulled his notebook out of his pocket and found a clean page. He wrote:

> You stole my heart,
>
> And you stole my pride.
>
> I had no choice,
>
> I stole your ride.

He tore the page from his notebook, folded it, and tucked it into Bea's door. Miles pedaled away, smiling and ringing the bell on the handlebars.

Drinks for the Ladies
Kevin Rabas

Before Miles left, Calvin took the cardboard coaster out from under his beer and wrote on it, circling the outer circumference ring. He gave it to Miles.

"She's not making it easy for us," Calvin said. "You might turn up the heat on her."

"How?" Miles said. "And why?"

"Prof, I love her, too. Just not all of the time anymore. Take the bike back. The address is on the coaster. See what she does."

Calvin patted Miles on the shoulder.

"Good meeting you, Prof." Calvin used a hard "o" like in loaf. "Don't worry about Bea. She'll settle eventually. You can bet on it."

Calvin stopped by the bar on his way out. "Two prairie fires for the ladies." He left a twenty on the counter. It was a lot to pay, but some jokes, some gestures were worth it. It was a gesture he learned from a singer-songwriter, Greg Brown, who called it playing the poet game. Calvin would pack his lunches the rest of the week.

Cal and Julie Get Coffee, the Qs
Kevin Rabas

Julie called. "Where have you been? I've missed you, Cal."

"So good to hear," Calvin said. "Let's go get some coffee."

Calvin didn't like coffee, only espresso. That shot of coffee was enough, the caffeine without the taste. He also loved tea. Getting coffee was what people did now, though, when they didn't know what else to do, when they didn't know how else to meet and be casual.

"I thought about calling," Julie said. "But I thought you would call. What's up?"

"I ran into an old friend. We caught up."

"Did you kiss?"

"Nah."

"Sleep together?"

"You mean have sex? No."

Julie was laying it on pretty thick, like Columbo. Calvin wondered if she was suspicious.

"Just got together," Calvin said. "Harmless. But it took time. Gosh, I'm glad I'm here with you. I don't have to think about the past or ghosts or what was."

"I have my Anthony. He emails me cute jokes and asks to get together. I usually say no, so I know what you mean. I know what he wants." She looked down. "You know what I mean."

Calvin took Julie's hand, said, "Let's spend the day together and forget about the past. We have something to create together. Let's spend the day at it. What do you say?"

Julie smiled an unaffected smile, a child's smile, and Calvin smiled back the same way. The questions were done, and they could start out unencumbered and fresh, like old friends looking at new things, like new friends that had heard of each other, like new water through the waterwheel.

Calvin said, "Do you ever like to look at fish?"

Coffee and a Clue

Mike Graves

"Hey, Miles, you mentioned you'd like to hear me play the drums sometime. I've got a gig in Topeka if I can get there, but I don't have the wheels. My car won't start. This girl I know usually drives, but she can't make it tonight. I was wondering if you could haul me there. I know it's asking a lot, but I'll pay for the gas."

Miles thought for a moment and decided why not? It might be fun, and he would like to hear Calvin play.

"Sure, Calvin, let's do it. I've long harbored a desire to be a roadie. Don't worry about the gas. I remember what it's like living on a grad student's wages. I'll pay for the gas."

So it was set. They walked from the campus to Mile's place, picked up the Cavalier, and drove to Calvin's to load up the drums. They hit the road at a little after six.

"The gig is at eight, so after we set up, we'll have time to grab a sandwich and coffee. It shouldn't take more than an hour or so to get there."

"Sound's good. Where are we going?"

"A little place called Lola's Café on Gage."

"I know Lola's. I interviewed a poet laureate there for a literary magazine. Lola's is a great place. Good coffee, comfy chairs, and a nice mix of poets, writers, and other edgy souls. Should be fun."

As they drove they talked, and by tacit agreement they never mentioned Bea. In fact, they didn't talk about women at all. They talked about grad school. Calvin lamented the long hours, the lazy students, the endless papers to grade, and trying to get by with almost no jingle in his jeans. Miles empathized, having been there, but he also grew wistful when he recalled the late nights rapping with other grad students, drinking wine, sharing writing with each other, and vowing to change the world with their mighty pens.

They talked about music, how Calvin started playing drums as a teenager in garage bands and later playing at high school dances and parties. He talked about the culture and the characters, and Miles suggested he turn these experiences into stories if he hadn't already. They talked about baseball, and books, and shared favorite authors, and the hour passed quickly. Miles pulled into Fleming Place and parked a few doors down from Lola's.

They carried in the drum set, and Calvin went about assembling the pieces. While he worked, Miles went to the counter and ordered coffee for each of them. The woman at the register waved away his money.

"On the house. The band drinks free."

"That's cool, but I'm not with the band."

"I know, but you drink free tonight, too, professor. Call it an overdue thank you."

Miles was startled. He looked at the young woman again.

"You look familiar, and I'm embarrassed. I'm sorry, but I don't recall your name."

The woman smiled and winked.

"See if it comes to you. Don't worry. I won't leave you twisting all night, but see if it comes to you."

Miles smiled back at her. She did look familiar. He knew she was teasing him, having fun, and he could play along.

"Are you a former student of mine? Why the overdue thank you?"

"Enjoy the coffee, professor. Stop back for a refill."

She smiled again. She winked again. Miles carried the coffees to the bandstand.

Miles and Calvin Go to the Gig
Kevin Rabas

Calvin turned his key in the ignition, and the car only clicked and clicked. No dice. No start. He wondered who he could call in this pinch. Not Bea. That might look like starting up with her again, after the other night. Julie was gone. His housemates were all at a gaming convention. Slim Sally was too much of a risk. Miles came to mind. They'd had a drink. He said he liked jazz. Calvin paced into his part of the house, looked at his drums in a pile, in a stack. He hated wigging out on gigs, never did that. He called Miles, and off he went with Bea's other man, older man, hipster Prof man.

At the gig, Calvin noticed Miles. Miles nodded his head, moved to the rhythm. He seemed into it. Calvin played a tune across the drums, when his solo came, a kind of melodic story for making peace, making amends. What he played was a song for a handshake, a song for male solidarity and friendship, cohesiveness. The 32-bar solo was not regimented or militaristic, but instead sang of youth, of work— and of that joy of young boys running about outside, watching and listening to the animals; there were the sounds of the birds (chirps on the cymbals near the bell) and the sounds of the dogs and deer and buffalo, the sounds of hooves and feet rushing across the plains, sounds on the tom toms and the snare drum with the snares off, single -stroke rolls that crescendoed and built, the herd moving upward and onward. There were many other things, expressible and inexpressible. Calvin let the drums do the talking. When Calvin looked over, Miles was not looking. Had he heard? Or had he heard and moved into his own reverie, unknowing, unknowing why he thought?

Calvin knew that soon he'd need to begin playing towards a song for Julie, for a progression, a story across the drums, without which he might lose sight of what he dreamed, what he wanted, what his subconscious knew. As the songs played on, and Calvin kept time and comped, his mind went to the future, to Julie, and to their plan to go look at fish.

That plan had been interrupted. Julie had returned to see her father. Her father said he had wanted to see her, and she left at once. Calvin hoped Julie would be ok, when she got back. He hoped she could focus, hoped she could study and finish the semester out with clarity and pluck. Calvin wondered if he was distracting her or if she was distracting him.

Calvin always got his work done, though. He'd never had trouble with that. He did what he loved first, and he worked late to finish the rest, to memorize the IPA symbols, to read the section of poems, to write on the student papers, to read the novel of that week.

Calvin wondered what Miles and he would talk about on the way back. It was always the return that opened itself to the greatest dialogue, after the show was done, after what could be said in music had been said, and the silence surrounded you with music-less, star-filled night.

Calvin and Julie Go Look at Fish
Kevin Rabas

When Julie got back, Calvin walked down to Williams Automotive and got his blue and white Chevy S-10 Blazer and drove and got her.

"Let's look at fish," Calvin said, and he drove Julie to the pet store. Julie said she liked the bettas, their long, whiskery blue and red fins. The store kept the bettas separated, each in a clear cup filled three-fourths full.

"They fight," Calvin said. "I've heard that bettas can live in just a little splash, a little puddle of water in Korea. When the tide goes, they're left in these little pools, and they can live there a long, long time. But they're territorial, the males, and they fight. They lose eyes, they lose their lives."

"Would you fight for me?" Julie said.

"Sure," said Calvin. "Who am I up against?"

"You know Anthony does write me love notes over email."

"For how long?"

"For as long as I've known him," Julie said. "I'm not sure it's really me he wants. He might just want someone."

"Someone?"

"Someone hot," she said, and laughed.

"Let me take you out to see Rocky Ford."

"The fishing place?" Julie said.

"Yes. Let's go."

Calvin and Julie Go to Rocky Ford
Kevin Rabas

At Rocky Ford, the water was high. The water rushed from the dam. The engineers were letting the water out. A great waterfall fell from the top of the dam down into the bottoms, down into the streams, now full of rushing white water.

Asians and truckers stood along the banks, their lines in the water. A man would pull his line back, with a fish, unhook the fish and tie on a thick, heavy weight, bait, and fling the line back into the rushing white water and wait, but not wait long, before another fish would hook, and he would pull it in.

An Asian woman had 13 big fish on a string, head to head, diagonal, they waited for her to take them into her truck and drive them home to cook and eat, all bass. When the water was high, like this, truckers would park their rigs, take two or three poles at a time, hold one and ground the others, and wait, and fish, and pull in slick, grey water fish after fish, Coleman lanterns yellow-orange hot and glowing, through the night. They would fish until dawn, then get into their rigs and drive on to the next town, their cabs full of fish, their drives full of peace, their minds full of rushing water, Natural water, mountain water, although they were in the plains, what they remembered was that kind of Rocky Mountain high of fishing and fishing, thinking they might run out of fish, but they never did. Like spawning season, when the dam was let out, the fish came and came; the stream of them never let up.

Further downstream, men sat in the water, thick brown inner tubes around their bodies, catching the fish as they hid among the rocks. These men could reach out and touch the fish. Some did. As the fish came to the lower water, they were easy to snag among the rocks. These men had bags of fish, leaders of fish on metal hooks and snaps with them. Fish and fish.

Calvin climbed up the concrete bank that led to the top of the dam. He held out his hand, and Julie took hold. Calvin and Julie looked down at the water as it hit the bottom, as it hit the stream bed, and they looked at the water fall all of that way, and if you looked hard enough you could see the dark bodies of the fish among the white, rushing water, the fish falling and falling, their heads up, their heads down, flying, it seemed, in clouds of rushing, white water. The fisherman could see what they would catch come to them, falling through air, falling through rushing, rushing water. Their weights, their heavy weights seemed light as bobbers in that hard, fast water.

Julie squeezed Calvin's hand. "Isn't it so terrible and beautiful?" she said.

Phoebe and a Refill

Mike Graves

"Hey, Calvin, see that gal at the counter?"
Calvin looked and nodded.
"Do you know her?"
Calvin looked again and shook his head.
"No, I don't think so. She's cute, though."
The band had taken a break. Calvin was settling in at his drums, getting ready to play a solo while the rest of the band gathered for the last set. Miles was impressed with Calvin's skill on the drums. He enjoyed watching Calvin immerse himself in the sound, eyes closed, swimming in another pond, dipping beneath the surface, coming up for air, and going back under again.

The band was terrific. They had a mellow, bluesy sound that the coffee crowd appreciated. A woman who went by the name of Cricket belted out throaty tunes of hard times and misspent lives.

Miles looked over at the woman at the counter. She was cute. She was a petite brunette with dancing brown eyes, and when she smiled, she had a dimple on her cheek. Miles sipped his coffee and tried to remember where he had known her. He tried to recall her name. He played the alphabet game. Did her name start with A? No. B? No. C? No. He got to F and paused and paused again at H but went on and stopped at P. He looked at the woman again and closed his eyes. That dimple. Miles remembered the dimple. Her name started with P, but it didn't have a P sound. P, P, P... aha, Ph. Her name started with Ph. He had it.

He looked at her and smiled. No wonder he didn't recognize her. The last time he saw her, she didn't look at all like this. She'd changed, grown more beautiful. The only thing that hadn't changed was that dimple, that terrific dimple. He strolled over to the counter.

"How about a refill, Phoebe?"

Phoebe laughed.

"We have a winner! One refill on the house."

"It's good to see you again, Phoebe. How's the little one?"

"The little one is fine, but he's not so little anymore. He's in kindergarten now and growing like a weed."

"Wow, kindergarten. I didn't realize it had been that long. And give me a break, Phoebe. You've changed a lot, too."

Phoebe laughed.

"Yes, I have. I was a mess back then. I'd still be a mess if it hadn't been for you. You haven't changed much, though. Maybe a little sadder around the eyes. How's everything in your world?"

"Still spinning. Sometimes my world wobbles a bit on its axis, but it's still spinning."

"Last time I saw you, you were a newly minted PhD."

"Well, now I'm a seasoned PhD, slogging on toward tenure."

"And is there a Mrs. Professor?"

Miles shook his head.

"No. There's no Mrs. in my world. How about you? Are you married? I've forgotten the name of your son's father."

"Don't worry. I haven't forgotten him, but I'm trying. He left just before my son was born. No, I'm not married. No matter. I'm happy as a single mom."

The band played, and they chatted. Cricket sang a Norah Jones tune called "New York City" and followed that with another Norah Jones tune called "Rosie's Lullaby." Miles and Phoebe talked about where Phoebe had been these past years and where she hoped to be someday. The talk came easy, and the laughter, too, and much too soon, the band played its final number. Miles looked at his watch and excused himself.

"Tonight I'm a roadie. Gotta help the drummer load his equipment."

Phoebe reached over and squeezed his arm.

"It was good to see you again, Miles. I've thought about you often."

"It was good to see you, too, Phoebe. Maybe I'll get back this way. If I do I promise not to forget your name."

Phoebe looked at Miles with a steady gaze.

"You won't forget my name again. I won't let you. Come back again. You won't forget my name, and you won't forget my son's name either."

Miles looked puzzled.

"What is your son's name?"

Phoebe smiled."Didn't I tell you? It's Miles."

***

"So, did you figure out who she was?"

Miles nodded.

"Yeah, it finally came to me. She's a former student. Her name is Phoebe. She took a couple of my classes during her senior year. She's changed a lot since then."

"How so?"

Miles and Calvin were headed west toward Manhattan. Calvin's gig had been successful, a good crowd, terrific tunes, and Miles had told him how much he'd enjoyed it. Now Calvin wanted to hear about the gal behind the coffee counter.

"She went through a tough time her senior year. She drank a lot back then, used drugs, that sort of thing. She got involved with a guy who used her, and she got pregnant."

"Sounds like you really got to know her."

Miles smiled.

"Yes and no. I don't know why, but one day after class she showed up in my office. We'd been discussing *Light in August* in class, and I figured she wanted to talk about Faulkner, but she didn't. She just started talking, telling me about herself, her life. Some of it was ordinary, some of it was beautiful... and some of it was ugly."

"So did you give her any advice?"

Miles shook his head.

"Nope, it wasn't my place, and I wouldn't have known what to say anyway. I think she just wanted to talk, and she wanted someone to listen. So I listened."

"Did she come back?"

"Oh, yeah, all through the fall semester and again in the spring until she graduated. She'd show up in my office, sit down, and talk. I never knew why she came to me, but she did. I've got a buddy who's a psychologist. He told me once that everyone needs someone to talk to. Everyone needs someone they can tell their innermost thoughts to without fear of judgment. He said that if everyone had someone to talk to, someone who would listen and not judge, not give advice, that psychologists would be out of business. We wouldn't need them.

He also said he had no fear of going out of business."

"Wow. She must have really trusted you."

"I suppose. I still don't know why she chose me to be her sounding board. Until tonight, I never saw her after graduation. She had her baby that summer. Do you know what she did, Calvin? She named her son Miles. It about knocked me off my pins when I heard that."

"That's awesome."

They drove for a few miles without speaking. Miles thought about Bea. He thought about Phoebe. He thought about serendipity.

"Thanks for asking me to drive you tonight, Calvin. I really enjoyed this."

"Hey, thank you, Miles. I was afraid I'd miss the gig."

"You know, I think Phoebe might want to see me again."

Calvin looked at Miles and started giggling. Miles glanced over at him, and Calvin laughed harder.

"What's so funny?"

"Man, for someone so bright, you can really be dim. Don't you get it? She pours out her life story to you. She shares her secrets with you. That's the most intimate thing a woman can do. And to top it off, she names her child after you. And you think she might want to see you again?"

Calvin shook his head.

"Miles, Miles, Miles."

Miles had to smile. He stared ahead at the road and smiled.

***

Miles read the sentence, stopped, and read it again. "Your Grace should know before all else that my name is Lázaro de Tormes, son of Tomé González and Antoña Pérez, natives of Tejares…"

He stopped and closed his eyes. He thought about the other night in Topeka, listening to the band, watching Calvin lose himself in his drums, and, of course, he thought about Phoebe. What a surprise it had been to cross paths with her. It was what, almost six years since he'd last seen her? She'd changed. Six years ago she'd been strung out on booze and drugs. Now she looked clean… and beautiful. What Miles remembered most about the other evening was the easy conversation, the ready laughter, and the way she held his hand while they talked. She'd squeezed his arm when he said he had to leave, a way of saying it was okay to go now, but don't forget to find your way back. Oh, come on, Miles thought. She just squeezed your arm.

He picked up the picaresque novel and read the sentence a third time. Fred Holland stuck his head in the door.

"What are you reading?"

Miles held up the book.

"*The Life of Lazarillo de Tormes*, except I'm not really reading it. Can't seem to focus."

He tossed the book on his desk.

"So if you're not going to read, do you want to go to lunch?"

Miles did, and a few minutes later they were in Aggieville, eating sandwiches in their favorite deli. Fred swallowed a bite of corned beef and wiped his mouth with a napkin.

"Miles, you seem to be preoccupied these days, always lost in thought. Is everything okay? Do you have a lot on your mind?"

"Yeah, I guess I do. Nothing bad though. I ran across someone I hadn't seen in a long time, a woman. She's been on my mind. I didn't know it showed."

"Miles, let me give you some advice. Don't ever play poker for a living. A poker face you ain't got."

Miles laughed and nodded.

"Fair enough, Fred. Thanks for the advice."

They ate their sandwiches, and the conversation switched to basketball. As they finished and stood to leave, the door opened. A couple of people left the deli, and a couple more came in. One of them was Bea. She spotted Miles and smiled. She walked over and put her hands on her hips.

"Well, well, well, if it isn't the handsome stranger. Are you the guy who stole my bicycle?"

Calvin Helps Julie Move to Chaucer House
Kevin Rabas

Calvin pulled his blue Blazer up to Julie's house, and Chain Lady brought out a pink laundry basket full of clothes with a boom box and a phone cradled on top, and cords bird-nested everywhere.

"Nice of you to help," Chain Lady said.

"Not a problem. I wouldn't miss helping Julie move."

"Cal, sweetie," Julie said. "You're a doll for moving me."

"He does look like a paper doll from the back, Jules," Chain Lady said.

Julie agreed. "Not much of a butt, but that's ok with me." She patted him in the behind, a quick, gentle schwack to the blue jeans.

After loading up the back and the passenger seat of the Blazer, Julie drove behind Calvin, her white Mercury with its red racing strip zipping along behind him. The window and moon roof were open, and Julie's sandy blonde hair ruffled and fanned in the wind.

Chaucer House was a yellow A-frame. Julie was on the top floor. Calvin carried the laundry basket and plastic milk crates and boxes and garbage bags up the wooden steps, around the corners and the landings, to the top floor, where Julie would have the top bunk.

"No steps?" Julie said. "How do I get up?"

"Pull yourself up," Caroline said, Julie's new roommate.

Calvin said, "I'll make you some steps. For now, how 'bout a step ladder?"

Cal and Julie got one at the Wal-Mart, a perfect fit. Leaned against the front of the bunk, it led up with the perfect amount of steps. A little rickety, Julie did look forward to some better steps.

Julie gave Calvin a big hug, when they were done lugging the stuff, after their quick run to get the steps.

She said, "Cal, you're the only guy, besides my Dad, who's ever helped me move."

"It might happen again," Calvin said.

"Here's to many, many more moves together," she said.

Calvin kissed her quick, and as he went home, he opened all the windows on the Blazer and let the wind tear over him. When he got home, there was a message on his phone. Julie said, "Let's get dinner, and you should see the washer and dryer here. Bring your clothes."

Green Bike Stolen, Again

Mike Graves

"Help! Thief! This man stole my bicycle!"

Bea gasped, mocking the role of a damsel in distress. A few heads in the deli turned, and a couple of people smiled before returning to their sandwiches and conversations. Miles had to laugh.

"Sit down, Bea, before someone has me arrested."

"Okay, okay. Don't leave, though. Sit with me, okay?"

"Yes."

Miles had been eating lunch with his colleague, Fred Holland. They'd finished and were ready to leave when Bea showed up. Fred went on ahead, saying he'd see Miles back at the office. Bea took the chair Fred had vacated.

"Hello, Bea. How have you been? I haven't seen you in a while."

"I've been around. You haven't called."

Miles raised his eyebrows.

"I didn't think you wanted me to call."

"Why wouldn't I want you to call?"

"Because the last time I called you were peeved at me, that's why."

"Miles, you worry too much. Sometimes you just have to go with the moment, you know? Do what you've gotta do."

"Bea, you're more difficult to read than Sanskrit."

"That's part of my charm. So why'd you steal my bicycle?"

Miles grinned.

"That's part of my charm. I don't know. To get your attention, I guess. A friend advised me to do it."

"Calvin?"

"Yeah, Calvin."

Bea stared at Miles. She twisted the bracelet on her arm, the silver and turquoise bracelet he'd bought her in Washington, D.C.

"Why don't we go to your place and jump each other like a couple of bunnies, Miles?"

"You're not long on subtlety are you, Bea?"

"Why be subtle? It's not like we haven't done it."

Miles considered the offer and the options. He had a class to teach this afternoon. He could cancel class, of course. Professors were allowed to cancel class once in a while. He thought about Phoebe then wondered why he was thinking about Phoebe. Bea interrupted his thoughts.

"Miles, quit thinking. The moment calls for action. What's it gonna be?"

Miles looked at Bea. She was, as usual, adorable in her understated, thrift-shop fashion way. He wanted her. He wanted to be with her. He wanted to hold her and kiss her and caress her and tell her he loved her and make love all afternoon and into the night. He ached for her. He took her hand and squeezed.

"Bea, sweetheart, thank you for the offer. It sounds wonderful, but I'm going to have to say no."

Bea looked stunned. Miles stood up and left.

***

"'A man like me is helpless,' Grant was saying. 'Just like a fly in a pan of molasses. There's no escape for him. The more he tears around the more liable he is to rip his legs off.'"

An apt simile, Miles thought. He felt the fly's pain. He was stuck, and he ached, and the more he struggled the worse he felt. He knew he'd done the right thing. He'd said no to Bea. He'd stayed strong. He just wished the right thing didn't hurt so much. Thoughts of Phoebe popped into his head. He'd thought of Phoebe earlier when Bea had invited him to bed, and now he thought about her again.

"What contrasts do you find in Hamlin Garland's story? How is 'Up the Coolly' a reflection of life?"

Miles thought about Phoebe's smile, her dimple. Her innocent smile and her knowing eyes lent her an air of mystery that made her attractive, desirable.

"Anyone?"

A young man, a senior, made the mistake of looking up from his book and glancing at Miles. The eye contact was brief but fatal. Miles called on him. The young man cleared his throat.

"Well, Garland presents contrasts throughout the story."

"True. Can you give us some examples?"

"Well, at the beginning he describes the valley. He uses words like 'majesty' and 'breadth' to show its beauty. Then on the next page he describes the town as 'sleepy and squalid.' The town sounds pretty ugly."

"Good, that's right. Very good."

The young man exhaled and slouched back in his chair.

"Anybody else? What other examples can you find?"

And so it went for the remainder of the period. Miles struggled to keep his mind in the classroom, but he drifted in and out. Garland's story was a study in comparisons and contrasts. Phoebe and Bea, Bea and Phoebe. Phoebe was no stranger to the seamy side of life. She'd lived in ugliness but had grasped a thread of hope and pulled herself up. Bea remained a puzzle. In her words, it was part of her charm. Bea was flighty and spontaneous, qualities Miles welcomed and seldom encountered in his life as an English teacher. Phoebe was raising a child on her own, exhibiting the maturity and steadiness Miles appreciated and admired.

"Look for other examples of contrasts in the story, everyone. Think of your own lives. Why do these themes remain relevant today? Anyone? Anyone?"

Another Gig at Lola's
Mike Graves

Calvin knocked on the door and leaned in.

"Hey, Miles, I wanted to let you know I'll be playing in Topeka again tonight."

"Are you playing at Lola's?"

Calvin smiled and nodded.

"Yep, that's why I mentioned it. We'll be at Lola's. Maybe Phoebe will be there, too."

Now it was Miles's turn to smile.

"Okay. Do you need a ride?"

"No, I'm all set. Julie and I are going together. Some other people we know may drop by, too, Miles."

"Oh? Like who?"

"Julie mentioned the gig to Slim Sally, and she sounded interested. She said she'd probably be there. Sally's been hanging around with Bea, you know. Just thought you should know she might show up."

"Thanks, Calvin, for the invitation and for the heads up. I'll try to make it."

Calvin waved and ducked back into the hallway. Miles went back to grading papers, but his mind drifted toward thoughts of Phoebe… and Bea. He hadn't called Phoebe since he'd seen her in Topeka. He wasn't sure why. He'd run into Bea at the deli, and she'd come on to him, but he'd turned her down. He wasn't sure why he'd done that either. Miles finished grading his papers. He read over his lesson plans for the next day, tapped out a couple of e-mails to students and colleagues, and locked the door to the office.

Miles had decided he would go to Topeka. It was only five o'clock, but he thought he'd drive over early and treat himself to an Italian dinner at Paisano's Ristorante near the coffee house. As he drove, images of Phoebe popped into his head, pleasant thoughts. Maybe she'd be in the coffee house when he arrived. Maybe she'd have dinner with him.

Miles made the drive and parked his Cavalier in front of Lola's.

He walked into the coffee house and looked around. Several people were sipping coffee, chatting, reading, or writing. Miles was disappointed when he didn't see Phoebe, but he cheered up when a guy behind the counter said she would be in later that evening.

"She's usually here by now, but she had to attend a teacher's conference for her kid."

Miles had dinner at Paisano's, but eating alone was a drag. He ate a salad with breadsticks and drank a glass of wine, but passed on an entrée. It was still early when he finished so he strolled to a nearby cigar store and bought an Arturo Fuente Hemingway. Miles sat in the smoking lounge with other patrons and made small talk. After about an hour he walked over to Lola's.

He looked through the door and saw Phoebe at the counter handing coffee to a customer. She made eye contact and waved. He walked in.

"Hi, Miles."

The greeting arrived in stereo, one from Phoebe to his right and another from his left. He waved at Phoebe and turned to his left. Bea sat in a chair next to Slim Sally. He waved to her, too.

Bea looked at Phoebe. Phoebe looked at Bea. Bea looked at Miles. Phoebe looked at Miles. Miles turned his head back and forth from Bea to Phoebe. Miles wondered, now what?

Pizza and the Underwear Incident
Kevin Rabas

When Calvin arrived, Julie had her hands white with flour.

"The washer downstairs is great. Take them on down. The Era's on the lid."

Calvin loaded his clothes into the new clothes washer. The white machine didn't even have that skim of dust on it that they usually do. He put in socks and pants and shirts and underwear, and he started the machine running.

Upstairs, Julie's hands and wrists and arms were covered in flour.

"We used to make pizza like this, when we were kids, all four of us. Johnny, Amanda, Star, and me."

Once Julie had the pizza flattened, they spread Julie's homemade sauce on it, then mushrooms, green peppers, onions, and cheese. One of the girls in Chaucer house was vegetarian, so they left off the meat. It was a big, big pizza. The round circle barely fit on the metal pizza pan. Someone in the back was cooking corn. Someone else had hot dogs boiling.

One of the house girls said, "He's cute. But remember, no guys sleep here. Have a guy over for the night, and you're kicked to the curb."

"That's Samantha," Julie said. "She's up with the rules."

When the pizza was done, the young women brought out everything from the kitchen, and blond crew cut guys and guys with dark closely shorn hair came in. Mike, blonde and blue-eyed, strong like an ox, sat down next to Calvin, and put his arm around Samantha. Samuel, dark-haired, in a navy jumper from the mechanics garage, said, "Hey, Julie," and tapped her on the shoulder, said, "I can fix those steps of yours up there. Hear you've got some trouble."

"Calvin can do it," Julie said.

"Don't say I didn't ask."

They prayed. They ate. Julie slipped down for a few moments, to shift Calvin's clothes into the dryer, and fold her own. When they finished eating, someone turned on the tube, and they all watched the Peanuts on TV, something wholesome, something without any cursing. Calvin thought he could get used to this, but then again it was late November in Manhattan, KS, 1996, and Tarantino films were out, and Calvin didn't know if he would want to go so long without *Reservoir Dogs* or *Pulp Fiction*. Though sometimes gruesome, and full of cussing, they captured the time, the place, the era Calvin lived in.

When Julie descended the stairs into the basement, they found Calvin's clothes folded, and a pair of his underwear duct taped to the basement rafter, a joke.

"At least they were clean," Calvin said.

"Those righteous bitches," Julie said. "This really pisses me off."

Calvin kissed her, but he didn't know if that really made it better. Calvin carried his clothes out of the basement. He went quickly home.

Praying, Faith, and the Drums
Kevin Rabas

A note card was taped to the door on his screened-in porch, a place he'd once used to shelter a friend's big husky dog. The card read: "See you at the gig tonight, sweet, sweet Calvin." Calvin packed his drums. He called Miles, told him Bea would be coming.

During the drive to Topeka, Calvin's mind was full of big, sweeping brush strokes, a sound subtle as snow falling in a gentle breeze, a Paul Motion tune feeling, sparse, minimalistic, meditative. Calvin wasn't sure what would come next. Julie was moving into the campus Christian group led by the Episcopalians, and she now was part of Chaucer House. Calvin was no joiner, but he might have to choose, he might have to join the campus group to stay with Julie, to be around. Calvin thought of God the way he thought of electricity. To him it was mysterious and powerful, and to most unknowable. Agnostic, but spiritual, Calvin believed what we learned of spirit and faith we had to learn through the self, mainly, through what we did, through what we thought. Calvin agreed with Kazantzakis and with D.H. Lawrence, God was inside each of us; we just had to wake Him. Somehow, Calvin thought, this might prove a rub with Julie's group. But, Calvin thought, Julie looked so full of light when she clasped her hands and prayed, full of heat on a winter night, she glowed. He'd seen this. He'd see it again. At the table, in Chaucer House, over her pizza and corn, Calvin peeked out at them all, hands folded. With one eye, he watched them; he watched them as they prayed.

Calvin prayed behind his drums. What he most wanted to say was beyond words, something the instrumentalists knew, shared—communion through music. Small group improvisation, jazz combos, through them Calvin prayed. And what he usually prayed in was a circle of joy, his hands, his body not quite his own, pulled and pushed by the other notes in the air, in the room. He played to accompany. He played to sing out, through drum head and cymbal hit. That's what he looked forward to tonight, his prayer. Also, some friends would be there. He wondered what he'd say to Bea. At first, Bea didn't really get into Calvin's gigs, Calvin's drumming. But she said once, perhaps in jest, that she'd like to marry a jazz bassist. A jazz drummer wasn't that far off; the two (drummer, bassist) played as one. Calvin remembered how, during an impromptu trip to New Orleans, he'd planned on getting Bea a wedding ring. She spotted it in the window, and wanted it. Calvin ended up giving her pralines.

Other Possibilities
Mike Graves

Miles sank into the overstuffed lounge chair and let the music wash over him. For a moment, for a brief, delicious few ticks of time his mind was at rest and there was nothing but the music. It was meditative. It was spiritual. It was peaceful and calming and at the same time energizing and alive.

Miles watched Calvin work the sticks, stroking the skins, urging the notes, almost as if he were freeing the beats from within the drums. Calvin appeared to be in a state of bliss, at once animated and serene.

The music stopped and gave way to enthusiastic applause. Miles opened his eyes and looked around, readjusting his mind to the present. The coffeehouse was crowded. Every seat was taken, every table was full, and several people were standing and milling around.

A few people waited at the counter for their coffees and lattes. Phoebe was behind the counter, mixing and serving drinks with quiet efficiency. She glanced at Miles and nodded. He waved and nodded back. He scanned the room and saw a few familiar faces, people he hadn't met but who tended to hang out and read, write and chat with friends. He noticed Bea sitting on a couch, visiting with Slim Sally. Miles had stopped by to say hello earlier. Bea had asked if they could talk later, and Miles had said sure, but Lola's had filled up so fast they hadn't had a chance.

The last swallow in his cup had gone cold, and Miles decided to get a refill. He waited for the line at the counter to go down, dropped his coat in the chair to save it, and walked over to Phoebe. She took his cup and filled it.

"So, Miles, is she your girlfriend? She's cute."

Miles smiled at her directness.

"You've been busy tonight, Phoebe. When do you get a break? I'd like to talk."

"I'll be able to take a break when it quiets down. You didn't answer my question."

Miles turned to look at Bea and noticed she was watching him.

"You know, Phoebe, I don't know the answer to your question. I thought she was my girlfriend. In fact, at one time I thought she might be the one for me. Now I don't know. I don't know what she feels for me, and lately I've begun doubting my feelings for her."

"Why is that?"

"I've decided to explore other possibilities."

"Oh? When did you decide that?"

Miles looked into Phoebe's eyes.

"Recently."

Miles returned to his chair. Phoebe's eyes never left him. Neither did Bea's.

Calvin and Bea and the Pralines
Kevin Rabas

Calvin walked downtown and bought Julie a necklace made of little blue stones and white shells. It looked fun, but classy. The string was black leather, not hemp. He wanted to give her something. When he paid, in cash, two twenties into the hand of the lady at the register, Calvin remembered the last time he'd given a girlfriend a gift.

The semester had just ended, and Bea and Calvin wanted to celebrate. Bea said John Woo, who was another English grad. student, and his girlfriend, Adria, had just headed down south to New Orleans, a week after Mardi Gras. Bea said John said they should join him. Calvin knew Bea liked John Woo, perhaps a bit too much, but Calvin thought the trip might do them good. Besides, Calvin had never been to New Orleans.

The drive took a day. Bea and Calvin bickered most of the way. When they pulled into town, Calvin parked out front of a hotel, and went and asked about a room. They said $200. The only room left was the honeymoon suite. Too rich for my blood, Calvin thought, and went back to the car. When he tried to back the car out and into the street, it wouldn't go back. He tried going forward. The car drove fine. He tried backing again. No dice.

"So we can only go forward from here," Calvin said.

"Your car's junked," Bea said.

"True. I'm worried, too. But if we only go forward, we're ok."

Calvin parked, and they went in. $200 was a lot, but they didn't want to risk it. Who knew what would come next with the car. Calvin carried Bea's red bags up the stairs to the room. The bathroom had mirrors on every wall, and a big big mirror over a Jacuzzi.

"That'll be fun," Bea said. "Go get the basket."

Bea had packed a wicker basket "for fun," she said. In it were chocolates and condoms. On his way back in, two slim guys in black leather jackets said, "Hop hop, Easter bunny." Calvin wasn't sure if they were joking in fun or joking to get a rise out of him. It was dark, and the street puddles reflected light, and Calvin knew this was not the best part of town. When he got in, he locked the door. Around the door, the striking area was worn and chipped off. It barely locked. Calvin pulled the dresser a little bit in front of the door. No use taking chances.

When Calvin got to the bathroom, Bea was already in the tub. She looked happy, and her skin was red. Her arms held the edge of the Jacuzzi as if she was in a hot tub. Calvin undressed and got quickly in. They kissed under the mirror. They fled to bed.

Bea chided Calvin about the dresser in front of the lock, in front of the door. "You're paranoid," she said.

"Just trying to be safe," Calvin said. "I might not be able to fight them all off of you. You're such a beauty, so damn enticing."

When they left in the morning, the Blazer would back and go forwards. Calvin thought, "A-Ok, so far." He planned to take the car in, when they could.

John and Adria met Calvin and Bea at the Russian Tea Room. Bea called and set it up. While sipping tea in the historic French Quarter, Bea put her hand on John's and told him how glad she was to be there, with them, on break, away from little Manhattan. On the brick street, listening to the musicians, kids with washboards, panhandling, and a slim woman with dirty blonde hair singing "Moanin'" by the black statue of Jackson on his horse in the square, a guy sitting on a battery-powered amp, playing guitar, his eyes closed, his singer touching along the edge of his shoulder when she came to the sexy sections. Bea put her hand in Adria's, and they skipped forward into the square. Bea gave the washboard kids coins. Adria gave Bea a peck on the cheek. Calvin felt alone. He wondered if he'd have to make the drive back alone. Bea was playful, but he wondered if it was much more than that. He didn't ask, but he started to know.

After the musicians, Bea came back to Calvin, held his hand. John and Adria held hands, too. The four walked by a novelty story with a silver crocheted wedding dress and a row of antique wedding rings on black velvet. Bea said, "I want one. I want that one," and Calvin thought maybe. Bea held Calvin by the waist and said "Please."

"But what would it mean?" Calvin said

"What do you think?"

When the group passed the candy market, Calvin decided that what he'd give Bea would be pralines.

Al Pacino Knows
Mike Graves

"Hey, lover, wake up."

Miles opened his eyes. He hadn't been sleeping. He'd been absorbed in jazz and coffeehouse chatter. It was getting late, and Calvin's combo was playing their last set. He looked up at Bea.

"Hi, Bea. How have you been?"

Bea stood with her hands on her hips.

"We need to talk, Miles."

"Sure, but it's a little loud. How about after the set?"

"How about now, outside?"

Miles wanted to hear the music, but Bea seemed determined. He stood up and put on his coat. Bea led the way outside to a bench near the coffeehouse. Miles nodded at Phoebe behind the counter as he walked through the door. The night was cold and quiet, and the fresh air tasted good after the stuffy atmosphere in Lola's.

"So, what's going on, Miles. Are you dumping me or what?"

Miles looked puzzled.

"Bea, I don't know what to say. You wouldn't talk to me over Christmas, so I backed off. Then when you did see me, you wanted me to sleep with you. I never know if you are hot, cold, or in between."

"Do you ever just live for the moment, Miles, go with the flow, let things happen? Does it always have to be so predictable with you?"

The words stung. Miles decided to change the subject.

"How was your Christmas, Bea? Was Santa good to you? Were you naughty or nice?"

Bea chuckled.

"That's what my mother used to ask me when I was a little girl.

Every year, just before Christmas she'd ask, 'Well, Bea, were you naughty or nice this year? Santa only gives presents to good little girls.'"

Bea looked lost in thought as her memories took her back.

"Then one Christmas when I was about eight or so, about the time when kids start doubting if Santa is real, I decided I'd had enough with naughty or nice. So when my mother asked the question, I just said I'd been naughty. I told her I didn't see why I should be nice 364 days just so I could get some lousy gifts on one day of the year. It didn't seem fair."

"Bea, you're something. What did your mother do?"

"Oh, she looked shocked and said I should be good, yada, yada, yada. But later I overheard her telling my dad what I'd said, and they both were laughing."

Miles laughed, too. Bea kept talking.

"Of course, later on, as I grew older, I discovered what all girls learn. The whole concept of naughty or nice is bogus. Nice girls may get pats on the head and teddy bears for Christmas, but naughty girls have all the fun."

"You're having fun with me now, aren't you, Bea?"

Bea leaned closer and whispered.

"I always have fun, Miles. I just can't understand why you don't."

Bea kissed Miles, first on the ear, then on the cheek, and finally a deep, long kiss on the lips. Miles closed his eyes and kissed her back. Warmth swept over him. Then a light, cold breeze slapped his face, and he opened his eyes. He looked toward the coffeehouse. A woman was watching from the door. Phoebe?

Miles stood up.

"I've got to go, Bea."

He rushed toward Lola's ignoring Bea's laughter behind him. Once inside, he asked for Phoebe. The guy behind the counter shook his head.

"She just left, man. Said she had a headache and went out the back door."

Miles punched a number into his phone, and when he heard the mechanical voice he left a message.

"Phoebe, please give me a call. I need to talk to you."

He waited several minutes and tried again. The same voice answered, and he left an almost identical message. He tried again a third time with the same result. He waited. Finally, after nearly an hour, he gave up. He looked at his watch. It was late, and he had to get back to Manhattan.

On the drive home, Miles thought about the evening. He had hoped to visit with Phoebe, but Lola's had a packed house, and Phoebe had been busy with customers. She'd only had time to smile and wave.

Bea had come on to him – again. Why? Miles couldn't deny that he felt something during their kiss. He wasn't over Bea, but he sensed she was just toying with him. Bea said she just wanted to have fun. She was long on honesty, but short on compassion.

***

Miles pulled up to the curb and parked his Cavalier. He went inside and poured a glass of wine and sank into his chair. He didn't want to think about Bea and Phoebe anymore. He opened a worn copy of *Wuthering Heights*. His advanced literature class was covering Emily Bronte, and he decided to prepare some discussion questions on her novel. He read for a while and began formulating thoughts to share with his class. Who did Catherine really love? If she loved Heathcliff, why did she marry Edgar? Who did Heathcliff love, Catherine or Isabella? How does a man fall in love with the wrong woman? Why do people who are in love with each other let each other go and marry other people? Is love worth fighting for? How does the novel relate to your lives?

Miles took a sip of wine and looked at his phone. There were no missed calls.

Miles woke up and sat on the edge of the bed and stared out the window at Saturday morning. A few flurries of snow wafted past the naked branches, but there weren't many, and they fell straight down.

Not much wind, thought Miles. Good. I need some exercise.

He washed up in the bathroom and dressed in sweatpants and sweatshirt. He stopped in the kitchen for a quick cup of coffee. He picked up his copy of *Wuthering Heights* but decided he just wasn't up to Heathcliff's antics. He opened the door and stood on the porch, breathing the cool air. He suddenly felt alive. He started to run off the porch, but he noticed a flash of chrome from behind the bushes.

Aha, he thought.

He pushed the evergreens aside, and there was the green bicycle. How long had it been since Miles had swiped the bike from Bea?

Long enough, he decided. Should I take it back to her? Why not? He would ride it to her place and jog back, a good workout.

Miles rode through the neighborhood and felt so good he detoured onto the campus. He rode between buildings and crossed a parking lot. Even though it was cold, the wind was quiet, and it was good to be outdoors. He left campus and pedaled through Aggieville, noting the empty bottles and cups on the sidewalks from Friday night revelers. He turned toward Bea's and pulled up on the sidewalk in front of her apartment.

Miles got off the bike and walked it to the spot behind the bushes where he'd found it. He leaned it against the wall and started to leave. A voice stopped him.

"So, the sneaky thief returns to the scene of the crime."

Bea stood in the doorway. She wore a bathrobe, and her hair was damp.

"You'd better get in, Bea. You'll catch a cold standing there like that."

Bea grinned.

"Do you care, Miles? Do you care if I catch a cold?"

"Of course I care. I always care about you."

"Then why are you ignoring me? Is it the woman from the coffeehouse? Have you found someone else, Miles? It seems like I asked you that question before, but I never got an answer."

"I guess it's because I don't have an answer, Bea. I just don't know."

"Poor, poor, Miles. So educated, so smart, and so clueless."

"You'd better get inside, Bea. Maybe I'll see you later. Let's have lunch at the deli."

Bea wiggled her hips, and her robe fell open. She was naked underneath.

"I can't wait for lunch, Miles. I'm hungry now."

Miles stared at Bea. He couldn't help himself.

"You're playing with me, Bea."

"Of course I'm playing with you. And I want you to play with me."

Miles wanted her. He wanted to be with her. It had been so long. Later, he couldn't remember walking up the steps. He had no recollection of holding her or kissing her in the doorway. He didn't recall stumbling into her living room with her in his arms. But he must have.

***

Miles stared at the ceiling. Bea slept softly beside him. At one time, making love with Bea had been joyous, a merging of two souls. At least it had been for Miles. Had it ever meant the same to Bea? Had they just made love moments earlier or had they just had sex? Miles enjoyed being with Bea, he couldn't deny it. But was la petite mort with Bea life affirming or soul denying?

"Miles, what are you thinking about now?"

Miles turned toward Bea. Her eyes were closed.

"Just thinking about us, I guess."

"And what are you thinking about us?"

"I think we are good together, Bea. What do you think?"

"I think you think about it too much. Let it happen, Miles."

Bea rolled over. Miles got up and got dressed. Bea propped herself up on her elbow.

"Are you leaving?"

"Yeah. Do you want to get together later tonight?"

"No can do, Miles darling. Sally and I are going to a Pearl Jam concert in Kansas City. We'll crash at my folks' place tonight."

"Fine. Have fun."

Miles leaned over and kissed Bea goodbye. He jogged toward his place and passed through Aggieville. The Campus Theater was showing *Scent of a Woman*. Miles bought a ticket and found a seat near the back. Al Pacino was playing Lt. Col. Frank Slade, a bitter, blind combat veteran spending a weekend on the town with a young aide named Charlie Simms played by Chris O'Donnell. Miles enjoyed Pacino, and he loved the role he was playing...

"Women! What can you say? Who made 'em? God must have been a fuckin' genius. The hair... They say the hair is everything, you know. Have you ever buried your nose in a mountain of curls... just wanted to go to sleep forever? Or lips... and when they touched, yours were like... that first swallow of wine... after you just crossed the desert... Hah! Are you listenin' to me, son? I'm givin' ya pearls here."

Women. Wine. Lips. Pearls. Miles walked home. He didn't sleep well that night. He couldn't turn off his mind. He woke early Sunday morning and lay in bed reading. After breakfast he tried calling Phoebe. No answer. He didn't leave a message. He read some more, turned on the TV, surfed the channels, and finally clicked it off.

Miles put on his coat. He got in his car and drove. He didn't think. He drove. The Cavalier was pointed east on Highway 24. A sign read Topeka 55 miles.

***

"Tall black coffee, please."

"Anything else?"

Miles looked around Lola's. It was quiet. A few people were reading or writing, tapping at laptops. He didn't see her.

"Eh, is Phoebe working today?"

"No, sorry, man. She's off today."

Miles nodded and handed the man a couple of bucks.

"She's usually home on her day off, though. You might give her a call."

"I tried that. She won't answer."

The man grinned.

"Yeah, she was pretty pissed the other night. Here, use my phone. She'll pick up. Talk to her."

Miles punched in her number. She answered on the second ring.

"Hi, Jason, what's up? Are you busy?"

"It's not Jason, Phoebe. It's Miles. Please don't hang up."

Miles listened to the silence and continued.

"Please let me talk to you, Phoebe. I need to talk to you."

"I thought you needed to talk to me the last time. Instead you went for mouth-to-mouth with your girlfriend."

"That's what I want to talk to you about."

Silence.

"Please, Phoebe."

"I can't come in today… you could come over, I guess."

"That would be great."

She gave him the address, and Miles handed the phone back to the guy behind the counter.

"Thanks, Jason."

She lived on Sunny Dell Court a few blocks south of 21st Street. It was in an older neighborhood and a little tricky to find, but Miles passed a school and a church and found it just off Eveningside Drive. She opened the door before he knocked.

"Hello, Miles."

"Hello, Phoebe. Thanks for letting me stop by."

Miles stepped through the door. A large, white poodle appeared, squatted on its haunches and lifted a paw.

"This is Apollo. He wants you to shake hands."

Miles bent over and took the dog's paw. Apollo barked once and retreated to another part of the house. The sounds of padding feet signaled the arrival of someone else. A small, dark-haired boy peeked around the corner and ducked behind his mother's legs. Phoebe bent down and kissed the top of the boy's head.

"And this is the rest of my family. Miles, meet Miles."

Fish Necklace, Acceptance Letter
Kevin Rabas

After the barrage of gift cards with hearts and crosses and hands held in prayer on them, he came to the jewelry aisle. Crosses and more crosses. Silver crosses, pink crosses, wheat-colored crosses, rhinestone crosses. Small crosses, like tie tacks, and crosses that had heft, weight, the Mr. T variety. Calvin thought, if Jesus came back, this is not what he would want to see, the instrument of his death. Jesus calls out to Papa, and they still tack him up—on what? A big wooden cross. Don't remind Him. Calvin found the row with silver fishes, metal ornaments. These were more peaceful. He bought the first one that struck him, silver with a black leather necklace band. She might like that. He passed on the holy spirit necklace. It looked more like the outline of Texas than a dove. Silver fish in hand, Calvin went to the register and paid, then put the necklace in his front pocket. When would he see Julie again?

Across the street, someone zipped by on a green bike. It didn't look like Bea.

Calvin wondered if he should write something to go with the gift. Also, there were those steps to work on sometime soon. He'd call his Dad, get his help, when he went home to visit. Dad was a carpenter.

It was just two blocks to Yellow House. When Calvin got there, he opened the black metal mail box on the front step. Inside was a letter. The return address was: Anke Essen, *Untamed Forsythia*. That was the journal she published. Inside was the note, in blue pen.

1 December 1996

Dear Calvin,

I not only liked your poem, I fell in love. I'd like to publish it in the upcoming issue of *Untamed Forsythia*, if it is still available. Please let me know ASAP.

Also, please check the enclosed proof for errors and send a current, short 1-3 sentence bio.

Thanks.

Sincerely,

Anke Essen

Editor

Calvin thought. A win! I need to call someone and go get a beer. Poet's payday. Although Calvin, in essence, would only be paid in one free contributor's copy, it was a win, a solid win, and with the odds of publication now being less than .05 to 5 percent for unsolicited submissions to most small press literary magazines, Calvin considered himself lucky. Uncovered, but lucky.

Are You My Dad?
Mike Graves

"Are you my dad?"
Phoebe got down on one knee.
"Miles, this man is Mommy's friend. His name is Miles, too, but he's not your daddy."
"Oh. Well, whoever you are, do you know how to play *Pigeon Trouble*?"
Miles looked confused and turned to Phoebe for help. She laughed.
"It's a *Sesame Street* game on the computer. Come on, Sweetie, I'll get you started. Maybe you can teach Miles how to play."
Phoebe's son sat down in front of the computer, and she reached over him and logged onto the game.

"You know I can't call you both Miles. How about if I call you Big Miles and Little Miles?"

Phoebe's son looked down.

"Does that mean I'm Little Miles?"

Phoebe looked up at Miles. He sat down next to the child.

"How about just calling me Miles, and we'll call you Big Miles? Will that work?"

The boy grinned.

"Yeah, I'm Big Miles."

While they played on the *Sesame Street* website, Phoebe made lunch in the kitchen. Pleasant cooking smells wafted through the house, and she called them to the table. They ate chili and rolls while Apollo, the French poodle, lay quietly in the corner.

"So what else do you like besides video games, Big Miles?"

"The zoo."

"The zoo is terrific. Do you go often?"

The boy bounced up and down.

"Uh huh. Our teacher took us."

"What's your favorite animal?"

"The tigers. I like the tigers."

He roared.

They talked, and they ate, and they laughed. After lunch they watched TV and took the dog for a walk and stopped at the school playground. Big Miles needed a push on the swings, but he wanted to do the slide by himself. Afternoon faded into dusk, and Miles had to get going.

"This was great, Phoebe. Thanks."

"It was fun. I'm glad you came over."

Miles knelt down.

"So long, Big Miles. Maybe next time we can go see the tigers."

"Yeah!"

Miles turned to the door, and Apollo appeared. He sat down and held out a paw. When Miles took it, the dog barked once and left.

"Apollo says, 'Ciao.'"

"A French dog named after a Greek god that speaks Italian. I guess that makes sense. You know, we never really got to talk."

"Sure we did. I don't have a claim on you. Your life is your business. But this was nice. Miles approves of you, and so does Apollo. I do, too. Come back."

Miles gave Phoebe a hug and left.

"Rawr! Rawr!"

"That's a great tiger roar, Miles. I'll bet that tiger is really afraid."

"Rawr!"

"Whoa! You're starting to scare me!"

Phoebe laughed, and the boy ran into her arms.

***

"Hey! There's the elephants! Let's go see the elephants!"

The boy ran ahead while Phoebe and Miles followed along. It was one of those special January Sundays when the gods smile, the sun shines, and memories of cold and snow fade into the gray recesses of one's mind. Miles had surprised Phoebe and Big Miles by arriving with a picnic lunch and tickets to the zoo. The young boy was so excited he could barely get his words out.

"First I wanna see the tigers! And then the giraffes! And the monkeys!"

He ranted on while Phoebe laughed and Miles led them to the car. Now they stood outside the elephant cage, and the small boy's excitement was contagious.

"Wow! They're huge! Is that a mommy or a daddy elephant? How come that one has bigger ears? Hey, there's the giraffes! Can we feed the giraffes?"

"Sure, Sweetie. Come on."

They walked toward the giraffes.

"Miles is a great kid, Phoebe. How did you become such a good mother?"

"On the job training, kiddo. Not a lot of theory involved here. I make my mistakes, and he does, too, but I never forget how much I love the tyke no matter what happens. And whatever happens never stops, twenty-four seven."

The giraffe's long tongue curled out and the leaf of lettuce disappeared from the boy's hand. He giggled and held out his hand for more. Phoebe placed more lettuce in his hand, and the boy watched the huge tongue do its work. When the leaves were gone, the boy stepped back from the cage and waved at the giraffe.

"I'm hungry, too. Can we eat lunch now?"

They walked to the playground across the street from the zoo. A number of children were already there, and the youngster gulped a sandwich quickly so he could go down the slide. Phoebe and Miles sat on a bench beneath a bare tree and watched. The sun was warm on their faces.

"It's nice of you to do this, Miles. It means a lot to both of us. Money's tight, and we don't get out much."

She turned to check on her son. He'd left the slide and was running across the playground toward a stone sculpture of an octopus.

"It's my pleasure, Phoebe. I wanted to see you, and I didn't want to waste this sunny day."

They watched the boy struggle to navigate up the octopus. He slipped at first but found a foothold and pulled himself up. Phoebe called out to be careful and shook her head.

"That boy knows no fear."

A gust of wind blew over the bench, and Phoebe pulled up her collar.

"Phoebe, I want you to know there's no place I'd rather be right now than here with you and your son."

Phoebe looked into Miles's eyes.

"Is that right, Miles? No place else?"

"That's right, Phoebe. No place else."

They leaned toward each other, and their lips met. They held their kiss for a moment. Later, they would try to recollect how long they'd had their eyes closed. Ten seconds? A half minute? Does romance speed time or bring it to a halt?

The first thing they heard was a child's scream. Did the scream belong to the boy or another child? The scream was followed by other screams and then voices, adult voices, pleading for help and imploring "Where's this child's mother?" A crowd began gathering as Phoebe jumped off the bench and yelled a single word, "Miles!" The crowd parted as she ran to the crumpled shape lying beneath the stone octopus.

***

"I need a small spine board and oh-two. Stand back please. Who saw this happen?"

The paramedic barked orders, and two EMT's reacted without comment. One hurried to the ambulance for supplies while the second knelt down and cradled the boy's head in his hands to stabilize the spine. Phoebe knelt beside her son but gave way to the paramedic who was running his hands over the small boy. She felt a hand on her back and turned to look at Miles. He looked worried, too, but tried to reassure her.

"He'll be okay, Phoebe. These guys know what they're doing."

The paramedic barked again, and an EMT made notes that would later be passed on to the emergency room doctor.

"Patient is unconscious but has an open airway. No signs of external bleeding. Left arm appears to be fractured. Heartbeat is steady and regular. Pulse is one forty."

The paramedic lifted one of the boy's eyelids and shone a small flashlight into his eye. He repeated the procedure with the other eye.

"Pupils are equal and reactive to light. Let's attach the oxygen."

The emergency crew continued to work. The crowd of people had grown, and several people milled about whispering and wondering "what happened" and "is he okay." The sun was dropping, and it had grown chilly. People turned up their collars and stamped from foot to foot, but most stayed and watched.

The paramedic put an air splint on the boy's left arm before leading the team in rolling the boy onto the spine board. They strapped and secured him for transport to the ambulance. Phoebe gave a quick wave to Miles and climbed into the ambulance with them. Miles watched the flashing lights and listened to the wail of the siren fade into the distance before getting in his car and driving to the hospital.

Stormont-Vail Hospital was just down 10th Street from the zoo, and it took only a few minutes for Miles to find Phoebe in the emergency waiting room. She was alone and crying.

"Oh, Miles, I feel so guilty. I looked away for just a moment. Why did this happen?"

Miles took her hands in his.

"Phoebe, this wasn't your fault. Children play, and children fall. You couldn't have prevented this. Where is he?"

"They have him in surgery. He was unconscious. I tried to talk to him. I kissed him. I wanted to hug him, but he was unconscious. Oh, Miles, he's all I've got."

Phoebe cried. Miles put his arm around her. The waiting room was busy. Families waited for news on loved ones being tended to behind steel doors. Children fussed. People shifted in straight-backed chairs and tried to get comfortable. Others thumbed through magazines and read out-of-date articles on topics that held no interest. People glanced at watches and then at the clock on the wall. A TV hummed in the corner, but no one watched it.

A pair of nurses strolled by.

"It never fails. A nice day in winter, and we get busy. One guy sliced his hand trimming his hedges. In January!"

"It's the full moon. I've got a forty-five-year-old woman who OD'd. Says she used to smoke marijuana back in the day, but she's been clean since. Her blood tested positive for seven substances!"

The women paused at the entrance to the emergency room. One tapped a keypad on the wall, and the doors opened and closed behind them. Miles and Phoebe waited. From time to time a doctor wearing blue scrubs would come into the waiting room, visit quietly with a family, and disappear again behind the steel doors. Finally, one of the blue-clad doctors approached Phoebe. He looked serious, but then, doctors always look serious.

"Your son is out of surgery," he said.

Brady in Love
Tracy Million Simmons

The days following his mother's death were a blur of people and emotions, emotions and people. The faces of his relatives, his neighbors, and past and present friends of his mother were many and they were one. He felt himself constantly nodding in agreement. Of course, he remembered. Yes, he'd only been knee-high. Sure, it was a blessing. Absolutely, she was a very special woman. She'd be missed. He'd be okay. Life was mysterious. Death was unfair, but inevitable.

Only Mary's face remained constant and in focus. He could not say which aunt made the ham sandwich and pushed the plate into his hands, insisting he eat even though he'd just polished off a slice of meat loaf and half the dish of cheesy potatoes, but he could say that Mary sat right by his side, her shoulder touching his the entire time, and snuck bites of the sandwich to help him through this time of sorrow every time his aunt turned the other way.

It was Mary who held his hand through the service, both in the church and at the graveside. Her body next to his was so constant in the days following his mother's death that he grew accustomed to her warmth, as well as her commentary. On the fourth day after his mother's funeral, Mary did not come to his bed, unbidden, in the dark of night. Brady's mind and body finally succumbed to tears and he did not know if it was the death of his mother that caused his sorrow or the absence of the girl he loved beside him. In that short time he had grown to believe that Mary belonged with him.

Without his mother to take care of, Brady found himself with time on his hands. His father puttered around the house, sorting drawer after drawer of paperwork, always with a look of concentration on his face. Brady's offers to help went without response. Once, his father assured him that he'd let him know if there was anything he could do to help, but it was just paper. Bills. Insurance documents. Legal matters that wouldn't be of interest to a teenaged boy.

Mary still came by daily to talk and sometimes she left Colin so that Brady could watch him while she shopped or did other things in town. She never invited him. He found himself waiting all day for time with her, be it minutes or hours. His mother's flower beds had never looked better. And Brady was working on another bicycle. His mother's old green bike, looking brand new, zipped in and out of the driveway and down the road and most often away, ridden by Mary who had commandeered it as her own.

Each time she left, she hugged him. Each time he put his arms around her, he would find his face closer to that space at the side of her head where her neck was hidden by her lovely, long red hair. Finally the day came when he could no longer restrain himself. He pulled his arms more tightly around her as she started to pull away. He put his forehead against hers and bent his knees to lower himself so that they were eye to eye. He kissed her full lips gently, but deeply. He breathed her in. Life had never tasted so sweet.

"Brady," she gasped.

He took this to mean he should kiss her again, but this time his lips met her jawline. Then he felt her hands against his shoulders. Her fingers were hard and bruising. She pushed at him and an icy cold gap grew between their bodies.

"Stop Brady," she said. "Just stop!"

"But I love you," he said dumbly. "Mary…"

She was already walking away from him. Running. She pulled her sleeve across her mouth as if she could so easily wipe him away. It occurred to him that she was angry. Or hurt. He couldn't tell which.

"Mary," he called. "Mary, wait!"

Green Bike Returned

Tracy Million Simmons

The green bike sat in Mary's driveway, untouched.

On the third day after she ran from his kiss, he dawdled at the mailbox, hoping he would catch a glimpse of her, hoping that she would give him the chance to apologize and make things right again.

He sorted through the letters, reading each return address line by line. He straightened the mailbox flag. It was noticeably crooked. He used his thumb to polish the embossed letters that spelled out US MAIL. He finally turned away, retreating back up his own driveway.

The hinges on the door to Mary's house squealed. It was Mary's mother. She stood on the top step, observing him.

Brady waited.

Mary's mother descended the steps and grabbed the bike awkwardly by the seat and one handlebar. It made Brady think she had not spent much time on a bicycle. She pushed it across the street and up the driveway, leaning so that the bike moved away from her body as she attempted to avoid the open kickstand.

When she stopped, taking a few moments to assure herself the bike wasn't going to tip over, she said gently, "Mary thought it was time to return it."

Mary's mother had a kind face. The lines around her mouth and across her forehead were full with exhaustion and sadness. Her hair had nothing of the fierce red color that Mary's had. He wondered if Mary's father had red hair.

"Listen," Mary's mother said. "I know this probably isn't going to help, but Mary would want you to know that it wasn't your fault. She's sorry... or she will be, in time... if she gave you the wrong impression. She's just... not in that place right now. It's not for me to tell you, but..." The woman looked at Brady long and hard and that's when he could finally see the resemblance. Mary had her mother's eyes.

Brady put his hand on the bicycle.

"I'm sorry about your mom," Mary's mother said.

He dropped his chin against his chest and ran his thumb over the shiny green paint.

"I'm sorry I've not been more neighborly. I should have

introduced myself, I guess. I should have..." Her voice trailed off.

Brady wasn't listening anyway. He pushed the green bike into the garage. Mary's mother was still standing in the driveway when he hit the button. The garage door lurched down via a rough, electric motor for the first time all summer.

Mary Leaves for College
Tracy Million Simmons

Mary left for college on a Tuesday afternoon. A man arrived driving a large Chevy Suburban. His hair was a faded shade of Mary's, which shone like fire in the sunlight. The man and Mary's mother spoke briefly. Colin came out and refused to give the man a hug. Later, Mary and her father made several trips in and out of the house, filling the back of the vehicle with boxes, a neon green suitcase, an enormous brown teddy bear, and a large, clear plastic bag that Brady guessed was full of bedding.

Brady watched all of this from his kitchen window. When Mary and her father closed the back doors of the vehicle and went into the house, Brady went outside and sat on his own porch, pretending not to pay any attention to Mary's house at all.

He didn't look up when they came out of the house again an hour later. He didn't turn his head in their direction as Mary hugged her mother and her little brother goodbye. He didn't watch the big vehicle back into the street, pause, and then start to pull forward, threatening to take Mary away from him for good. But when the vehicle stopped, only a few feet from where it had started and the passenger door opened again, he was on his feet, almost running down the driveway as Mary came rushing toward him.

He didn't question; only held her in his arms and let her hold him back. Her head was on his shoulder, facing away from him. He closed his eyes and let the world stand still, determined to commit this memory of her in his arms to his mind forever.

"I'm sorry," she said, when she finally pulled away, and the words that poured from her mouth were at once nonsense and incomprehensible. He couldn't help but feel that they were lines from a bad after-school special. "You're so special, Brady," she said, and "Someday you will find a girl who deserves you...

"I'm not that girl.

"I never meant to send you mixed signals.

"I thought you needed a friend.

"I didn't mean to confuse you."

He found himself nodding his head in agreement, but his ears couldn't seem to tune in to the sound of her voice. Instead, his eyes took in the perfect form of her lips. His nose picked up the strawberry scent of her hair. Every nerve in his being felt the heat from her body, even as she turned and walked away from him, again.

This time, the vehicle did not stop.

Jake's Bike Shop
Tracy Million Simmons

At the start of the fall semester, Brady drove the old Ford F150 pickup truck his father had bought him to campus every day. Brady had thought that college would make him feel different, that he would somehow feel more like an adult or that he would suddenly have purpose or direction to his life. He envied the students who had come from other towns, who were living on their own in the dorms or in apartments near campus for the first time. Though Brady's father was rarely home, he still felt like a child each day he returned to the empty house. He would throw a frozen dinner in the microwave without even looking to see what it contained. He would sit at the kitchen table and study each night with the curtains wide open, watching Mary's house for signs of what she might be up to.

They never came.

In November, he put the green bike into the back of his truck and drove it into town. Downtown, near Aggieville, he'd seen a sign in the window of Jake's Bike Shop. "We Buy Used Bikes," the sign read. Brady parked the truck and lifted the bike out, gently running his hands across her handlebars. For a moment he considered throwing it back in the bed of the truck and driving it home, but his mother didn't need the bike anymore and Mary, it seemed, wasn't coming back for it. When he pushed the bike into the shop, nobody appeared initially. Brady looked around. He thought he detected the smell of jasmine. His mother had grown a jasmine plant in her bedroom. He wondered if his father had been taking care of it. He made a mental note to check on it when he got home.

"Hello?" Brady called into the shop, seemingly filled only with bicycles in various states of repair and disrepair.

"Out in a minute," a voice came from the back room.

Brady parked the green bike and inspected the short row of new bikes that were lined up near the window.

Many minutes later, a man came out from the back room, zipping the front of his mechanic's jumper as he approached Brady and extended his hand.

"I'm Harley. What can I do for you?" the man, whose nametag read Stan, asked.

"You buy bikes?" Brady asked.

Harley's face lit up when he saw the bike and he whistled. "Classic Schwinn," he said. "That there's a beauty."

Brady felt his chest puff with pride and he again contemplated taking the bike back home with him.

A sound of a crash came from the back room.

"You okay, Bea?" Harley yelled over his shoulder, bending to inspect Brady's handiwork.

"I'm good!" a woman's voice he recognized called back.

Brady watched as his English prof walked into the room. She wasn't really a professor, he knew. She was a graduate student, a teaching assistant of some sort, but Brady was still a freshman and considered everyone who stood at the head of his classrooms professors because somewhere he'd gotten the idea that's how things were when you got to college. You no longer had to deal with teachers. You had professors who were cool and liberal and, just as often as not, encouraged you to call them by their first name. He'd never called Bea anything, of course, because Brady was the student who sat in the back of the classroom and watched out the window, daydreaming about a girl named Mary, even as the attractive Bea, who tended to dress in thrift store clothes, did her best to engage him in the subject of English Composition 101.

"Well?" the man said.

"Oh Harley," Bea answered, giving Brady a wink. "Give the boy a hundred. It's a beautiful bike."

Bea was running her fingers across the seat, admiring the perfect green paint job, causing the hair on Brady's arms to stand up.

Harley was frowning.

"Look," the man said, turning again toward Brady. "Fifty is usually my absolute top dollar for a used bike, but I'll give you seventy-five. You've fixed this one up good, after all. I'm not going to have to do a thing to it."

Brady found himself nodding. Next thing he knew, the man was pressing a wad of cash into his hands. Harley and Bea fawned over the bike, seeming to quickly forget that Brady was there at all. He stuffed the cash into his pocket and turned to leave. The bell on the green bike jingled as he walked out the door. He turned his head just enough to see that Bea had straddled the bike and was flicking the bell joyously, her head thrown back in laughter.

She was no Mary, but the image of Bea on that bike made him smile.

Brady walked deeper into Aggieville, thinking maybe he'd come across someone he would recognize from school. He had money in his pocket and time on his hands. "Time to move forward," he heard his mother's voice in his head. "Time to move on."

24/7

Mike Graves

Phoebe stared as the surgeon spoke. She struggled to process his clipped, jargon filled speech. She puzzled at words like "concussion" and "subdural hematoma" and "compound fracture" and "abrasions." What did these words mean? What did they have to do with her son lying somewhere alone behind those cold steel doors? She felt insulated, trapped inside a giant snow globe, unreachable. Words approached her but couldn't get in. They bounced off the invisible glass and fell away.

Miles put his arm around her.

"Phoebe? Phoebe? Phoebe!"

The gray doors whooshed to a close behind the surgeon.

"Miles, oh, Miles, my baby, my poor baby."

Miles held her while she cried. When her tears stopped, she wiped her eyes and nose with a tissue.

"I didn't understand a thing he said."

Miles led her to a chair and sat down beside her.

"It's going to be okay, Phoebe. Miles is out of surgery and will spend the night in ICU. He bumped his head and had some bleeding inside, but it's stopped, and he'll be okay. He broke his arm, and they put a cast on it, and it'll heal fine, too. He has a few scrapes, but nothing else that's serious. The good news is that he's young and healthy, and the doctor says he'll be back to normal in a few weeks. He just needs to rest for a while."

"When can I see him?"

"As soon as they move him to ICU. You can stay with him tonight."

"I'm so glad you're here, Miles."

She squeezed his hand.

"I'm glad I'm here, too, Phoebe."

It wasn't long before a nurse appeared to lead Phoebe to her son. Miles gave Phoebe a hug and promised to call the next day. He watched her disappear behind the doors.

The sun had set hours ago. The night air was cold, and a wind blew out of the northwest. As Miles drove home he thought about the day, the warm, sunny day. He thought about the joy of a boy roaring outside a tiger cage and the terror of a mother watching her son being lifted into an ambulance. The three of them had had a special day together until poor little Miles had fallen from the stone octopus. Miles recalled Phoebe's words. It never stops, twenty-four seven.

As Miles neared Manhattan, he checked his cell phone and saw that he'd missed a call. It was from Bea. Now what, he wondered. He found out when he got home. The green bike was leaning against the porch. He shook his head. It never stops, twenty-four seven.

New Steps 1
Kevin Rabas

Calvin turned the key quick, started the Blazer, and sped across town, his windows down, the winter air coming and coming in. When he got to Chaucer house, Samantha, in her Lucy from the Peanuts haircut greeted him at the door.

"She isn't here. But you should see her new steps."

"Her what?" Calvin said

"Come."

Samantha led him upstairs to Julie's room. There were four thin 2x4 steps out of pretreated blonde wood with thick bolts and large metal washers and nuts as big as Calvin's thumb

"Samuel made them," Samantha said. Calvin remembered the wiry mechanic, another beau. Samantha gave Calvin an evil grin

"Didn't get to them soon enough, did you? Quickness and

attentiveness are strong virtues," she said

"I'm not sure these will even hold her—long." That didn't sound right, but it was true. Calvin climbed the steps quickly. They creaked with each step. Calvin brought out his pocket notebook and scribbled a quick note.

"Ok. Thanks, Samantha," Calvin said. "Sorry to bother you. Thanks for letting me in, showing me this."

When Samantha had him at the door, Calvin said, "Shalom."

Dead Air

Mike Graves

She was lying in his bed. Naked.

"Well, hello, lover. Long time, no see."

Miles felt a jolt of excitement. It had been a long time since he'd been with Bea. He fought to maintain his composure.

"Hello, Bea, and goodbye. This can't happen. Not now, not tonight."

"What's the matter, dude? Don't I excite you anymore?"

"Yes, as a matter of fact you do give me a rush. But when I'm with you I feel like a yo-yo on a string. I'm up, I'm down. I'm tugged this way, and then I'm tugged that way. I can't live like that, Bea."

Bea made a fake pouty lip.

"What a disappointment you are, Miles. You're no fun. You're way too serious. What have you been up to anyway? It's after midnight. Don't tell me you've been chasing after that barista in Topeka. Is that it, Miles?"

"Her name is Phoebe, and she had a really scary, bad day today. So did I. I'm exhausted, and I'm going to bed. Please leave, Bea. I'm too tired to argue."

Bea pulled the covers up under her chin.

"No way, dude. I rode the bike over, and I'm not riding it back home tonight. I'll freeze to death. You're stuck with me tonight whether you like it or not."

"Fine. Suit yourself. I'll sleep on the couch. Good night."

Miles pulled a blanket out of the closet, grabbed a pillow from the bed, and headed for the couch. It wouldn't be a great night's sleep, but at least he'd wake up without a cloud of guilt hanging over him.

His cell phone woke him in the middle of the night. He struggled to open his eyes. As he reached for the phone he noticed the clock on the table. It read 8:17. It wasn't night at all. It was morning.

"Hello?"

"Good morning. It's Phoebe. Did I wake you? I thought I'd call with a report on Miles."

Bea stood in the hallway. Naked. She had her hands on her hips. She called out.

"Hey, lover, I can't find a clean towel."

Miles put his finger to his lips, but it was too late. The voice on the phone cracked.

"Who is that, Miles? Who are you with? Oh, God. Do mean to tell me that after spending the day with me and my son you had the balls to run home to her? What is with you? What kind of person does that? I thought you were good. I don't know you at all!"

Bea walked into the room.

"Hey, I'm freezing here. Where do you keep the towels?"

Miles spoke into the phone.

"Phoebe, wait! Don't hang up. Please. I can explain. Phoebe?"

But he was speaking into dead air.

Calvin Runs Laps, Sally Joins
Kevin Rabas

Since Julie wasn't home, and Calvin felt like burning off some steam after seeing Julie's new steps, Calvin drove to the campus recreation center to run some laps. Calvin kept a pair of shorts and shoes in the back of the blue Blazer in a cloth grocery bag along with a padlock. That way, he could go whenever he felt like it, without thinking. Just jump in the car and go to the gym.

The track at the K-State recreation center is above the main room. You can run laps and look down and see people on treadmills, their legs pinwheeling above a black band, and you can watch as strong men push bars up, grunt, then lower the bars down again, and repeat. They clap their hands, white chalk up in a cloud, when done.

There's a red LED clock above the track. Calvin kept track of his time. He tried to hit 1:15 or less each lap, 8 times around for a mile, which added up to about a 8:30-minute mile. Not bad, for a quick jog.

He was almost through when he heard a jingling sound, bells. Slim Sally trotted up to him. She had on a hot pink top and black umbro shorts with pink piping.

"Wanna race me a lap?" she said. She shot him a toothy grin.

"Last lap," he said. "You'll win."

"Try me, sport," she said, and they sprinted.

Slim Sally was fast, but Calvin still had will, and was warmed up. Their legs pumped and pumped; Sally's legs blurred completely. Sally was ahead at the line, but she turned just as she was about to beat him, stepped into his lane, and caught hold of him. It was a kind of runner's hug.

"Gotya!"

"Ok, ok, you win," Calvin said. It was kind of funny.

"What's new, slick?" she said. "You look kind of beaten."

"Oh, it's nothing."

"How about the poetry? What news?" Slim Sally said. "I'll bet you're knocking them dead, winning this and that. You might even win that Silver Quill, when we graduate. I think Bea will get the Purple Hat of Presumption, and I'll get the Black Beret of Black Heart Angst."

"I did get into Anke Essen's magazine," Calvin said. "A win."

"I've always thought you were destined for good things," Slim Sally said. "This is just the first. When I teach Composition I at the community college, I think one day we'll open our *Norton Anthologies*, and there will be one or two of your poems."

"Really?"

"I really think I will. Good job, Calvin." She pecked him on the cheek. "And don't forget me, ok?"

"Ok," Calvin said.

"And who's this Julie, anyway? I kind of miss seeing you with Bea."

Calvin and Slim Sally Talk about Julie, Body
Kevin Rabas

"Julie's a pre-art therapy major. Our moms knew each other from work at the paper. I know what you're thinking, arranged marriage. But it's not that. We just seemed to hit it off."

"Is she thin?"

"Petite maybe. Pretty. I call her my little chickadee."

"Cute. Maybe a bit lumpy, but cute."

"You can be mean."

"Girls are mean. Don't you know that?"

"I guess guys don't think about it much, maybe. We're too busy bashing each other's brains out on the field, in the locker room, behind the church."

"Let me know if she doesn't work out, huh?"

"Who do you like?"

"I don't like anyone. I just like the best."

Slim Sally ran a hand through her long hair, turned.

"Later, sport. Good luck with your little chickadee."

Calvin ran three more laps. When he opened his locker, he turned the fish necklace over and over in his hands. He forgot about bringing it in. It had just been in the bag. Would she like it? What would she say? Calvin drove back to Chaucer House. She'd have to be home by now, he thought. Didn't the good Christian girls of the house have a curfew?

Calvin Gives Julie the Fish Necklace
Kevin Rabas

Calvin put the silver fish necklace into Julie's hand, and she closed her fist around the necklace. The black band dangled from her small hand like a loop. Julie kissed Calvin, and through the kiss Calvin could feel her joy, electricity in her lips.

"Thanks, Cal," Julie said. "This is so sweet, so sweet of you. Where did you get it?"

"Lauflin Christian Books & Gifts. Downtown. When I saw it, I thought of you. Of your joy, your faith, your spirit. I take it you like it alright?"

"I love it. You know my Dad got me a holy spirit tag for my bumper. It's silver, too, but it looks like the outline of the state of Texas. I'll keep it on, though. I want him to know I appreciate the gesture, the attempt. This, though, is wonderful. Beautiful and sweet."

"Like you."

"I hope." Julie started the black loop around her neck.

"What should we do to celebrate?" Calvin said.

"First help me get this on."

Calvin did, and he hugged her when the clasp closed. She leaned back into him, and they stayed that way, as in the sweetheart hold in square dancing, their arms together, him behind her, and Calvin felt a breeze from the wind come through Yellow House, up over his bed and past his computer and over the bougainvillea plant in its rope hanger.

Julie said, "But it's 9:30. I need to get home, sweets. How about tomorrow?"

"I'll bring you coffee. Americano?"

"Americano."

Calvin looked at the computer screen when Julie left. A blank page was up. His bed was made. The plant was watered. There were no distinct sounds from the street, only the buzz of cars on the blacktop. Then laughing and heel clicks. And men joking. Students walking from the dorms to Aggieville. Calvin felt, at once, alone.

She's Gone, Dude
Mike Graves

Miles called Phoebe, and he listened to her recorded voice instructing him to leave a message, and he begged into the phone for Phoebe to return his call, and Phoebe didn't return his call, and Miles called again. Every half hour. Then every hour. Then every few hours. He called Lola's Coffee House, and the answer was, "Phoebe's off today," or "Phoebe is taking care of her son," or "I haven't seen Phoebe."

This went on for several days, until that day he tried to phone her, and he heard the recorded voice say, "The number you have tried to reach is no longer in service. If you feel you have dialed…"

Miles drove to Topeka, anxious for what he would find, afraid of what he wouldn't find. Even as he pulled to the curb in front of Phoebe's place, he could see she was gone. The place was empty. Curtains were down, windows were bare, circulars and flyers littered the porch. She was gone. Miles looked in a window knowing what he would find. Bare floors, furnishings gone, Phoebe gone, gone, gone.

Miles sat on the porch with his elbows on his knees and his head in his hands, staring at the cold, gray cement. He sat for a few moments, and not knowing what else to do, he drove to the coffee house. Jason was behind the counter, and he didn't even wait for Miles to speak.

"She's gone, dude. She packed up and left. What did you do, anyway?"

"Do you know where she went, Jason?"

Jason dunked a couple of mugs into soapy water and shrugged.

"Tell me, Jason, please."

"Hey man, she swore me to secrecy. I can't talk."

"I've got to find her. I'm going to find her."

"She's gone, and she's not coming back."

Miles mulled it over. Phoebe didn't want to see him. Fine. But would that make her pull up stakes and leave? No. She wouldn't leave town because of him. Something else. Her son, Miles. She left town because of Miles. She needed help while Miles recovered. Who would she turn to? A friend? No, her parents. She went to be with her parents. Where did her parents live? Phoebe never mentioned.

"She went to stay with her parents, didn't she, Jason? Where do her parents live?"

Jason hesitated.

"I can't say, man."

"Jason, you don't have to tell me where Phoebe went. You don't have to back out on your promise. Just tell me where her parents live."

Jason grinned.

"You're kind of sneaky, aren't you?"

"I love her, Jason."

Nothing was said for a long moment. Miles waited. Finally, Jason grinned again.

"I guess it won't hurt to tell you where her parents live, but you're not going to believe it. They retired near their old alma mater. They live in Manhattan, dude."

A Detective with an Incentive

Mike Graves

He tried the phone book first, but in this age of cell phones and paranoia, many people either didn't have land lines or they had unlisted numbers. Her parents weren't in the book. He called the KSU Alumni Office, and, yes, they did have records for the parties in question, but contact information was confidential and couldn't be released over the phone. Sorry.

Miles thought it over. He'd find her. He knew he would, but how? He thought some more. The coffee houses. He'd check the coffee houses. Phoebe would have to work, and she was an experienced barista. She'd look for similar work in Manhattan.

There were a number of coffee houses in Manhattan, and Miles decided to start his search in Aggieville. He got lucky. He struck out at Starbucks and again at Radina's, but his third stop was at the Bluestem Bistro, and there she was, standing behind the counter, mixing a latte and chatting with a customer. He watched her work. He decided to hang back and not rush her, but it wasn't long before she noticed him.

They looked at each other for a long moment. Neither one moved. Miles wondered if she would speak to him. Then Phoebe smiled and shook her head from side to side.

"I figured you'd find me, but not this soon. What are you, a detective?"

"No, not a detective, just a man with an incentive."

"Oh, yeah, what incentive?"

"I had to find you to tell you that I love you, Phoebe. I had to find you."

Phoebe dropped her shoulders and looked down at the counter.

"You have a strange way of showing affection, Miles. You spend the day with me. You sit with me and comfort me on one of the worst nights of my life. Then you go home and sleep with another woman. How am I supposed to interpret that?"

"Phoebe, I can explain. Can you take a break? Can we talk alone?"

Phoebe asked her partner to take over for a moment and they slipped outside.

"Okay, Miles, talk, but I don't want to hear anything but the truth. No lies, and the truth had better be good."

Miles told her everything. About finding Bea in his bed that night, about letting her stay while he slept on the couch, about not wanting to play Bea's games, about how he couldn't stop thinking of Phoebe, about how he'd fallen in love with Phoebe, and on and on he talked, and Phoebe listened, and she looked into his eyes, and she put her finger on this lips and told him to stop talking, and he did. And they kissed. And they held each other. And a little piece of Miles melted inside.

Phoebe laughed and spoke in a Bogart voice.

"Of all the coffee joints in all the towns in all the world, you walk into mine."

Miles answered in his Bogie style.

"Sweetheart, I think this is the beginning of a beautiful friendship."

John Woo and Calvin Drink
Kevin Rabas

"She gone?" John said.

John Woo came in the front door with a bottle of Black Death (cheap) vodka in one hand, a full brown grocery sack in the other. John set everything down and took off his black leather coat.

"Man, did you notice? It's hot in here?"

"Doesn't seem hot to me," said Calvin.

"I'm dyin'. Here open this, and find some shot glasses."

Calvin spun the black metal cap off the vodka. Calvin hadn't really seen John much since New Orleans, and he wondered why he'd come. John Woo left for the bathroom, once the stuff was set down, and Calvin noticed that he was wobbling a little when he walked. There was a code in Manhattan. Cops picked up drunks and people almost drunk, wobblers. Calvin figured that's why John Woo had really ducked in. Calvin lived less than two blocks from campus. His house was easy to find. Yellow House was on the way. Also, John might have something to say. After the piss stream sound stopped, John came in.

"Man, I just gotta say, 'Sorry about New Orleans.' I didn't know Adria'd come on to Bea. It's like her though. She likes everyone, loves everyone."

"How can you keep up."

"I can't. She left."

"Sorry, man. Sorry about her."

"I think I saw a petite little beauty leave when I was coming in. New girl?"

"She's a nice little lady. Julie. She has a curfew, though. Church girl."

"I see. Never known that kind. Not sure I want to. Drink up!"

Woo passed Calvin Samsa the small glass, the shot, and Calvin drank.

Woo had a sandy colored biker mustache, with the two catfish-like strands coming down from the lip, coming down from the face. Up top, he was bald. Although he looked white, his father was Chinese. John had that fat Marlon Brando look of *Apocalypse Now*, with his bald head, his girth, his beard, his partial jowl. John was about 30. He wasn't fat, but he was robust, probably 250 pounds. John wrote well. Calvin thought he'd make it. John wrote fiction, and he also wrote a column for the school newspaper. As a graduate student, and a kind of home-made genius, John's columns were the best in the paper, examinations of culture, thought and art. His editors kept telling him to dumb it down, write for the 14-year-old reader. Calvin knew John liked Bea. Perhaps this is why he came, for his blessing.

The two drank and drank. They told stories. John and his friend Phil had dug up a coffin in the local cemetery last week. They took the rings, the jewelry. They put the coffin in their front entryway, for kicks. Phil was also bald, but skinny, and always carried a weathered brown briefcase with him, a philosophy doctoral student. John knew how to have a good time. Phil made the money for the exploits. Phil put in garage openers and sold pot on the side. John drank until he couldn't stand or sit and laid down on the floor. Calvin put a blanket over him, polar fleece. Calvin tucked him in. Calvin looked through the brown paper grocery bag: three new lighters (cheap ones), a loaf of French bread, humus, Doritos, French onion dip, Coca-Cola in a small bottle, a small pipe, and a hand-sized Ziploc bag of pot. Another reason to duck in. John had almost gotten caught. Calvin considered calling Bea and having her pick up John, but he thought better of it. Calvin went into the other room and began to write. He dimmed the lights. Let John sleep. Sleep it off. Dream of New Orleans, if you like.

Calvin Writes Julie, John Woo Sleeps
Kevin Rabas

Dear Julie,

Part of my past sleeps on my apartment floor, an old friend, John Woo, a guy from my first party days here in this little town, Little Apple, and all I want now is a little slice of quiet, time without—the past, the papers, the poems, the hours of class, and what I want is some blue silk sheets filled with you, no reminders of where I've been, who I once was—no memories of parties or empty shot glasses, but you and Kansas fields of wheat, their small hard grain and their tulle whiskers around us, around us in the sun.

Love, Cal

Marry Her
Kevin Rabas

"Where's the girl," John Woo said, when he woke up. "She's not here."

Calvin waited. "What girl?"

"That girl. Your girl," Woo said.

"I don't know if she's mine. But I think she claims me."

"Yeah. Your girl." Woo waited. "Maybe you should get her a rock."

"Marry her?"

"Why not?" Woo got up and got his brown grocery bag. He picked up the vodka bottle and handed the long black bottle to Calvin.

"Think on it. Use this if you need to," Woo said.

And Woo went, slow out the door, then quick onto the sidewalk and across the street.

Calvin Gets the Ring Money
Kevin Rabas

Calvin had $800 in the bank. He'd been saving it since he was little. He worked at the pool, as a lifeguard, and he vacuumed the pool early mornings at 5. He'd been a kid magician, performing at birthday parties for littler kids with his sister as his assistant. It paid better than mowing lawns. Calvin wondered if it was too soon to ask Julie. There was some competition, but Calvin didn't know if he should let that influence him. Then again, the first to open a small black box with a ring and a rock usually won, usually married, usually lived happily or not so happily ever after. Calvin would gamble. He'd go to the ring store and see what they had. Manhattan had one jeweler, Stine's, and Calvin decided that he'd go and look on Tuesday after class. Calvin was all about jumping, when it was time. He didn't mean to rush, but his life might be short. And young women might move on, might ditch, might hitch with someone else, if one waited too long. School was a kind of love catalyst. In between classes, houses, lives were decided. You looked the way you looked to attract. You used your brain to answer the questions, but you used your eyes to decide who you'd leave class with. It had been this way with Bea, as well. He spotted her early, and she honed in on him. He wasn't the first, but he outlasted most of the other young men. Now, he'd moved on, and Calvin might be creating a life, making a home. Calvin knew Bea hated Julie, and this act might nail the point home to Bea; Calvin was gone. Bea was sure to do something rash, Calvin knew. But Calvin couldn't think of her. He had to think of Julie. That was what mattered now. "Should I stay or should I go?" Calvin thought of Julie by the waterside, of taking her small warm hands in his. Calvin though of the calls to Julie, when her father was in trouble, his heart wearing out. Calvin thought of roaming the streets of Aggieville, hunting for Julie on Halloween night. "Why not?" Calvin thought. "If I must marry, why not marry a good Christian girl, a young woman of the Lord?" Calvin didn't know how much he believed in all of that, but Julie did, and she had enough belief for the two of them. Calvin drove to the bank. He took $800 out in cash. He took the envelope with the bills home and put the envelope in a drawer. He stacked some photos of Julie on top of the envelope. He had a few days. The money was there, when he was ready. Calvin picked up the phone, called Julie.

Green Bike Redux

Mike Graves

The healing began. It took more than a day, more than a week, but it began. It was easier with Phoebe in Manhattan and working right in Aggieville. Miles stopped by the Bluestem Bistro during the day, and if it wasn't too busy, Phoebe would sit with him. The talks helped, long talks over coffee about work, and school, and living with her parents, and wanting to get an apartment, and should she get a puppy for Big Miles.

Big Miles was healing nicely, too. His six-year-old body, like most bodies that age, was tough and resilient and quick to repair itself, and although Miles still wore a cast on his arm, that, too, had become unexceptional and rarely slowed him in kickball or prevented him from scaling the upper reaches of the playground monkey bars. Both Miles and his injured arm generated excitement upon arrival at his new school in Manhattan, but with kindergarten attention spans being famously short-lived, it took only a couple of days for both the boy and his plaster cast to be suitably inspected and admired and relegated to the ordinary.

Phoebe and Miles went to a basketball game in Bramlage Coliseum, and a slam poetry festival at Porter's, and they watched a movie at the Campus Theater. They attended a reading in the English Hall and ate chicken marsala at Della Voce, and Miles met Phoebe's parents and found them charming.

Some evenings Miles would serve dinner for Phoebe in his home. Some mornings he would serve breakfast. People grew used to seeing the two of them together, and colleagues who once inquired, "What are you doing this weekend?" began thinking of them as a couple and asked, "What are you and Phoebe up to this evening?" Tongues that once wagged and wondered fell silent, and like the small boy and his injury, the concept of Miles and Phoebe as a couple became commonplace.

Miles found himself thinking about Phoebe during the day, and more than once during his lectures he would chide himself for checking his watch and glancing at the clock in the back of the room. As the semester wore on and the unusually mild January faded into February, store and window displays became shades of red, white, and pink in anticipation of the lovers' holiday. Miles wanted to give Phoebe something special for Valentine's Day.

He began shopping early in the month, not wanting to wait until the last minute. He wanted jewelry, but he didn't know what exactly. He browsed a couple of stores, and one clerk in particular seemed impatient with his indecision, but another clerk in another store said just what he needed to hear.

"Don't worry. When you see what you want, you'll know it. Take your time."

And he did. He looked, and he waited, and he looked some more, and then it hit him. There it was. A diamond ring that not only sparkled but spoke to him, "Pick me. I'm the one." Miles bought it and had it wrapped and thanked the clerk for her help.

Another week until Valentine's Day. Miles thought he would burst with excitement, but he remained patient. He didn't let on, he didn't discuss the upcoming holiday with Phoebe, and he didn't ask her what she wanted. He waited.

Another thought hit him. He wanted to get something special for Big Miles, too. The little guy was getting along fine now, and Miles wanted something to celebrate his recovery. He didn't know what he wanted, but he remembered the clerk's encouraging words. He shopped and waited and shopped some more. And on the second day, there it was. And just his size. It was perfect. Miles bought it and carried it out of the store and hid it in the trunk of his car.

When the day arrived, Miles surprised Phoebe by suggesting that she come to his home for dinner. "And bring Big Miles." Phoebe had expected something romantic, of course, but she was pleased by the invitation that included her son.

Phoebe laughed when she saw the table. Candlelight and glow sticks, cabernet sauvignon and grape juice, grilled shrimp and hot dogs, wild rice and steamed vegetables next to macaroni and cheese. Miles bowed and waved at the table.

"Welcome to Chuck E. Cheese at Top of the Mark."

Even Big Miles laughed, mostly because his mother did. Dinner was delicious, and it was during dessert, chocolate mousse and cupcakes, that Miles laid the box next to Phoebe's plate. She looked at it and then at Miles. He didn't speak, he just smiled. Phoebe's hand trembled, and when she opened the box her eyes were moist. She took out the ring and put it on her finger.

"Oh, Miles, it's beautiful."

"Let me see, Mommy."

Phoebe turned to show her son and then turned back to Miles. He cleared his throat.

"Will you...?"

"Yes, yes, yes."

They held each other for a moment. Then Miles took her hands in his.

"I have something else. Follow me."

Phoebe and Big Miles followed him into the living room. Miles opened a closet door and lifted out the gift. Big Miles jumped up and down.

"A bicycle! A bicycle! Mommy, it's a bicycle!"

In short order, everyone had put on coats and hats, and the bicycle was wheeled out the door. Amid admonishments to stay on the sidewalk, the small boy began pedaling. Phoebe watched her son and took off her glove so she could admire her ring. Her eyes went back and forth from the ring to her son.

"Oh, Miles, he just loves it, and so do I. This ring is gorgeous. You put a lot of thought and love into this. Thank you."

She squeezed his hand.

"The bike is perfect, too. Look at him go. How did you know his favorite color was green?"

The Ring
Kevin Rabas

Julie rushed into Chaucer House and held out her hand. Samantha picked Julie up with one big hug and said, "Congratulations, girlie. You're gonna be a bride. When's the date?"

"Summer," Julie said. "Right after Calvin's birthday, August 1st."

"How'd he do it?"

"He asked me out to a romantic dinner at Bambino's, that little Italian place out North. He passed me an envelope. In it were a love poem and a flattened origami box. I opened the box, and inside was the ring, sparkles, light. He got down on his knee, cuing the music. A jazz flautist came from the wings. She played and he read the poem to me. People turned. People stopped. They raised their glasses, a slosh of red wine, and we kissed." Julie looked down. "Just think, in a few months, we'll be able to go home together, start our new life."

"Where's the big man now?" Samantha said.

"He's out getting chocolates. He said he'd be back by in an hour. We're going out. To a party."

An Invitation
Mike Graves

Miles tapped the card on his thumb and wore a puzzled look. Phoebe waited for him to speak, and when he didn't she reached over and squeezed his hand.

"Earth to Miles. Earth to Miles. What is it, babe?"

"Sorry. I got this invitation in the mail. Actually, we got this invitation in the mail. It's addressed to me, but it mentions both of us."

"And?"

"It's to a party. Friday night. It gives the address and time, but it doesn't say who's throwing the party. No name at all."

"That's weird. Just toss it. Let's not go."

Miles thought it over.

"It does mention entertainment. Calvin and his group will be playing. I dig his sound. Maybe he's behind this. Anyway, he's good, and the party's in Aggieville, so we could stop in. If we don't like it, we could leave."

Phoebe kissed him on the cheek.

"That's what I said, babe. Let's go."

Miles laughed.

"There's no name, no number, no RSVP. I love a mystery. Okay, we'll go."

***

"The weirdest thing happened today."

"What's that, babe?"

"I saw Calvin in the hallway today, and our conversation was strange."

"How so?"

Miles and Phoebe sat on the porch. It was cool, but the afternoon sun warmed their faces. Big Miles rode his green bicycle up and down the sidewalk. The training wheels had lasted only a day before he begged to have them taken off. Now he was an expert, flying down the walk, yelling "Look at me!" each time he went by.

"I was coming out of my office, and I saw Calvin. He was excited about something, but he wouldn't say what it was. He promised to make an announcement at Friday's party."

Phoebe brushed Miles's cheek with the back of her hand.

"That doesn't sound so strange, Miles."

"Well, there's more. I told Calvin I looked forward to hearing him play the drums at the party, and he looked puzzled. He said, 'I didn't know I was supposed to play. I thought you were going to read some poetry.' I said I didn't know anything about that, and I asked him if the party was his idea. He said, 'No way, I thought it was your party.' How strange is that? Calvin looked happy, though, really psyched up about something. He said we'd find out Friday."

"Miles, do you think we should go to this party?"

"I don't know. I confess something feels odd. Still, I think it would drive me crazy if we didn't go."

Big Miles rode by and let out a whoop. Phoebe snuggled closer.

The Party
Kevin Rabas

Julie pulled a spoonful from her ice cream and held the cold milk sugar on her tongue in her mouth until everything melted, then kissed Calvin and said, "Where are we going?"

"A party," Calvin said.

"Whose?" said Julie.

"It's a mystery."

"A what?"

"A mystery. The invitation didn't say. I am a little worried. (It said bring drums.) I think it's from Bea."

"Bea?"

"Yep. Bea. This might be her last big shindig, last dance, last night in the spotlight."

"When's her birthday?"

"I think today."

"I've got a few drums in the back. Just a few. If things get strange, I can pick the skins and shells and stands and cymbals all up and go, in just two trips." Calvin looked ahead at the road. Night was coming on fast, like a purple sheet coming down on the town. The lines on the road were shifting from bright white in twilight to blips of white and grey, to streaks in the darkness hit by headlights.

"One trip with me, sweetie."

"One trip with the help of my lovely, beautiful, kind fiancé."

Julie kissed him. Calvin put his right hand on her knee, and Julie moved his hand to her lap. Calvin's father drove trucks for a while, and he taught Calvin how to drive easily, with no effort, with one hand.

Calvin parked in the darkness. He kissed Julie and slung drums over his shoulders. The entrance to theater was only about 40 steps. Someone had turned a warehouse into a stage for garage bands years ago, and here they all were, coming in with drums and kegs and coolers and brown grocery bags full of quick things to eat--chips and nuts and humus dips. Just outside the entrance, Bea stood in a blue party dress. Strapless and shiny, with tulle at the bottom, like a ballerina's, Bea looked like a grown princess to Calvin. She beamed. She waved. Calvin lifted one arm and waved back. His drum bobbed.

Julie followed close behind with the rest of the gear. She was right. One trip, and they were in.

Inside, John Woo had his hand in a fish bowl. He pulled an orange goldfish from the bowl and held it over his mouth.

"Nice fish," Julie said

"Guess its name, and I'll spare it," John said.

"Sparkles? Orangeade? Annabelle Lee?"

"Calvin," Woo said, and he let the fish drop into his mouth.

Calvin set up his drums quickly, and, satiated, Woo unlatched a black guitar case, unwound a long black cord, plugged into an amp, and said, "So what should we play?"

Calvin said, "How bout *Misty*?"

Woo didn't get the joke. The young woman with the flute came over, said, "How bout it?" She launched into a quick, quirky but melodic introduction to the tune, then soloed. Calvin backed her on brushes. He used press taps, quick and vigorous but mezzo piano, to keep up and comp with her, but also to give her that subdued duet feel. Woo turned his back, tried to tune his guitar.

"Now where do I know you from?" Julie joked, and the young flautist quoted a phrase from the engagement tune. She knew the key. She knew where she could put the notes and fit it with what she had flowing now, the tune like a stream, quick but slight. Woo grumbled, started in on "Copperhead Road" alone. The flautist and Calvin ended, and Bea came over, in a rush.

"Was that *Misty* I heard?" Bea said.

"Sure was," the flautist said. "I'm Skye. I used to play for the school with Calvin. John Woo said I should come."

"Pleased to meet you, missy," Bea said. "Where'd you learn how to play like that?"

"I taught myself," Skye said, "listening to LPs over at the jazz library. I hiked over as a high schooler. They have a lot of Basie records here, Mann and Most on lots of them, but I like Eric Dophy better. Corea's Joe Farrell is also transcendent. It's hard to mark where one comes from, especially when I'm still learning, still very much alive. How about you? How'd you learn you should teach, should write, should be a scholar?"

"I've always loved books. My brothers would go into the fields, and I'd be left at home with my mother in the kitchen, with dishes, with dusting. When I was done, what was there to do? I read books. They held places, places I wanted to go. Paris, New Orleans, Prague,

Dublin. I've been to some of them now."

"New Orleans was something," Calvin said.

"Darling, it was." Bea twisted a silver snake ring on her finger. Woo brought her a glass of wine, which she swigged half of in one gulp. "You never really loved me, did you, Calvin?"

"You know I did," said Calvin. He tightened the nut on the cymbal. He spread the brushes so the wires were even, uniform. Bea drank the last of the glass.

"No you didn't. You don't know how to love. And Julie here will know it. She'll know it soon enough. And then good luck."

Julie was turning red. Something averted a showdown, though. Someone came into the room, and that stopped Bea. She turned her attention to an older man, walking swiftly in, a kind of older joy in his face and in his step. It was Miles, and someone was trailing him.

A Birthday Party

Mike Graves

"Hey, what's today's date?"

Phoebe told him. Miles gripped the steering wheel and shook his head.

"How could I be so stupid? How could I forget?"

Phoebe turned toward him and placed a hand on his thigh.

"Forget what, Miles? Why are you upset?"

"Oh, Phoebe, I just realized what this party is about. Today is Bea's birthday. I completely forgot. This is Bea at her best. An air of mystery, a little enticement... Stay close to me tonight, OK?"

"Don't worry, babe. I intend to."

They arrived at the address, a converted warehouse and saw several people carrying refreshments. A few were toting instruments and amplifiers. Miles pointed.

"There's Calvin. The dude with the guitar is John Woo. I haven't met the gal carrying the case. Looks like she plays a clarinet, maybe a flute. Anyway, the music should be good, and there's food and drink. Let's not worry about Bea, Phoebe. What's in the past is in the past. Let's have fun."

They climbed the steps to the warehouse cum theater. Calvin had finished assembling a hi-hat, and John Woo was tuning his guitar. The woman was laughing and started blowing softly on her flute.

Calvin picked up his brushes and accompanied her in a rendition of *Misty*. Miles didn't want to interrupt, so he gave Calvin a wave. Calvin acknowledged him with a flick of his brush and went back to his music.

Across the floor Bea stood amid a circle of men who were no doubt wishing her a happy birthday. Each tried to be wittier and more charming than the next. Bea tossed her hair and laughed and flirted, at ease as the center of attention. She wore a blue dress and looked stunning and knew she did. God you are some woman, Miles thought. Phoebe stood at his elbow and followed his gaze.

"She is beautiful, Miles."

Miles nodded.

"Yeah, and so is the black widow spider. Just ask the male spider right before he's led to his execution."

The lights dimmed and couples eased onto the dance floor. Miles squeezed Phoebe and they joined the others.

"I have a confession to make, Phoebe."

"I'm not sure I'm up for another confession, Miles. What is it now?"

"I just wanted you to know I didn't really want to dance. I just wanted an excuse to hold your body close to mine."

Phoebe giggled.

"I can live with that."

They danced a couple of numbers, and then the music stopped. Bea had the microphone in her hand.

"I have a special request. How about a little improv tonight? We've got a great band, and I'm going to ask a dear, old friend to take the microphone and read a poem. Miles? Where's Miles? Miles, come up here and recite something. Calvin and the group will play along in the back. Give Miles a hand, everybody."

There was a smattering of applause. Phoebe looked at Miles.

"Did you know this was coming?"

"No, no I didn't. It's OK, though. I'll say something."

Miles moved toward the microphone. Calvin gave him a nod.

"Speak, dude. We'll play along."

Miles cleared his throat.

"This comes from a trip I took last summer. I call it Eureka Springs Blues."

Calvin swished his brushes lightly over the drums, and Miles began:

She settles into a rhythm

in the mottled shadows of the catalpa blooms,

unmindful of too thick ankles

and too taut Capri's

and the Birkenstocking, flip-flopping crowd strolling by.

John Woo plucked his guitar, and the woman blew the flute.

From the band shell the harmonica wails,

and the bass fills in the bottom

and the brass soars in the sky.

She lowers her lids

behind rose-colored granny glasses

perched beneath silver pin curls,

and as finger-snaps brush her thighs,

she sings those,

I'm hanging on

to what's already gone…

blues.

Miles nodded and another smattering of applause followed. He gave the microphone back to Bea and headed back to Phoebe. Someone else began speaking as the band improvised in the background. Miles and Phoebe walked toward the bar. They each had a glass of wine when they turned back to the floor. Bea came toward them.

"Thank you, Miles. That was nice."

She turned to Phoebe and stuck out her hand. Miles noticed she wore the silver and turquoise bracelet he had bought for her.

"Phoebe, I don't think we've really met. I'm an old friend of Miles's. I'm Bea."

Miles noticed someone standing behind Bea, a woman. Miles couldn't see her face, but she seemed vaguely familiar. He moved a little to his left, and the woman shifted a bit. Their eyes met. A hollow thump punched him in the gut. He feared his wine might come back up. What was she doing here? He thought she was gone, gone forever, a part of history. Now, like rust beneath the paint, she had reappeared. Bea. Why did you do this, Bea? Bea smiled, enjoying the spotlight.

"I suspect Miles has told you all about me, Phoebe. Here's someone else from Miles's past, another old friend you should meet. Phoebe, this is Wanda."

The Party Continues Even After They Leave
Kevin Rabas

Calvin stirred that soup, swished his brushes round the drum head, spun and spun time in circles. When he looked up to see what was up with Bea, he saw Miles, and Miles looked caught and tired and worried, like he might bolt. A new woman was behind Bea, a woman in her mid thirties, with auburn hair that looked like early autumn maple leaves, and she had fire in her face. She smiled, but what she held was more than warmth; hot spite. She raised her voice. Bea did the same. And Calvin caught a bit of what they said above the tune, about the brushes and the flute, above bass, above guitar: "Neither of you ever knew how to love anyone, and now you've run to a little barista, and Calvin's run to runt, short and stout, a tea pot of a girl. You two know how to pick 'em." Calvin fluttered his brush, a kind of quick ending, the brushes cymbal hit, cymbal fade. He started packing his drums, not knowing whether Julie heard or not. But he was going, either way.

"What's up, slinger?" Skye said.

"The conversation's getting poisonous over there. It's Bea's party, but I'm going. You guys can handle it without me. Sorry."

When Calvin had the drums and hardware, cymbals and stands packed, he called Julie over.

"Are we leaving?" she said.

She hadn't heard Bea. Good, Calvin thought.

"Yeah. Bea's getting out of hand. Can you help me schlep this stuff?"

"Sure, slinger."

She had heard that.

Like a small bird, something flew past the band. Then a sound. Glass. Bits of glass, a crash. A wine glass had been let go.

"You never loved me," Bea said again. She was at the back of the band, drunk, yelling.

Calvin said, "You may be right. Neither of us may know what love is, as the song goes."

Skye kicked that tune. Bea swung at Calvin, and he ducked. Calvin took Julie's hand, and the two quickly moved, like two alpaca, loaded with gear and drums. "Yeah, get on out with your little woman. I always knew you'd leave me for her."

Calvin said, "I knew it was all over when I saw that bike. Goodbye, Bea."

And the night greeted the lovers, loaded with drums. Streetlight lit the sidewalk. Calvin helped Julie into the blue Blazer. Calvin quickly put the drums into the back, and they pulled out into the street, quick, before Bea could come, glass in hand, hand on hip, stumbling; she watched them go.

Into the Night
Mike Graves

Phoebe glared at Bea, and Bea returned the glare, sipping wine and rocking just a bit. Bea drained the goblet and hurled it over their heads, past the band. A tinkle echoed off the brick wall. Few people noticed until the music stopped and the band began packing instruments.

Wanda smoldered beside Bea, unable to contain herself. She shrieked at Miles, "You miserable slime, hopping from bed to bed like a toad on lily pads. You disgust me."

Miles shrugged.

"Nice to see you, too, Wanda."

Phoebe chuckled. Bea ignored her.

"I'll bet you wonder how I knew about Wanda and you, don't you, Miles?"

"Not really."

Bea ignored that, too.

"I found out at the bike shop, Miles. I was having my bike repaired. You remember, Miles, the bike you stole from me? The bike you used to ride to Wanda's house while her husband worked in the shop?"

Miles went back. He remembered the bike. What had Bea said to him about that damned green bike so long ago? What had she said that day she came to his office? He was busted, that was it. She'd told him he was busted. She told him he'd been spotted riding the bike in the wrong neighborhood. But who did she say had seen him? The guy at the bike shop? That was it. The guy who'd given her the bike. Bea had been cagey, but Miles recalled that long ago conversation.

"The guy who gave it to me saw you riding it."

"Is this guy your boyfriend?"

"That's none of your business."

Suddenly, he knew. He knew who it was. But he couldn't say his name, wouldn't say his name. It wasn't fair. He'd give Bea a chance, a chance she would never give him.

"Back off, Bea. Stop right now. Let's walk away from this and pretend it never happened. I'm taking Phoebe and going home."

Bea cackled. "No way, dude. We're riding this pony to the finish line. I've known about you and Wanda for months."

"That was long ago, Bea. Before I met you, and before I met Phoebe. You've held it over my head, waiting for a time to use it. Only tonight isn't the night, Bea. Stop. Stop it now."

"Or what, Miles? What are you gonna do?"

Miles wished someone would split his head with an ax and make the pain stop. Bea wouldn't relent. "Please, Bea. You're playing with people's lives. You told me a guy saw me riding the bike in Wanda's neighborhood. You told me it was the guy who gave you the bike. I didn't realize until tonight why that guy was also in that neighborhood. Let's drop it, okay?"

Bea wobbled, and Wanda steadied her.

"What's this about, Bea?" asked Wanda. "What guy are you talking about? Who gave you the bike?"

But Wanda knew. Call it intuition, call it insight, call it what you want. She knew and continued, "The guy at the bike shop. The guy you're talking about: It's Jimmy, isn't it? You're talking about Jimmy. Why would my Jimmy give you a bicycle, Bea?"

Bea glanced from side to side, looking for support. She didn't find any.

"Answer me, Bea."

Miles took Phoebe by the hand and nodded toward the door. "I can see you two have a lot to discuss," he said. "We'll say goodnight."

Miles and Phoebe headed for the exit. Wanda began ranting like a talk show host, calling Bea terrible names. Outside, Miles started to speak.

"Phoebe, I—"

Phoebe laughed. She burst into loud, hysterical, belly-busting laughter. Miles was confused. He didn't know how Phoebe would react to the evening's events, but he never expected this.

"Oh, Miles, I'm not laughing because it's funny. It's never funny when people get hurt. I'm laughing because it's absurd. Life is absurd. Sometimes it's funny, sometimes it's sad, sometimes it's painful, but it's always absurd. I love you, Miles. I love you, I love you, I love you, and I want to be with you for as many crazy, absurd years as you'll have me."

"I love you, too, Phoebe."

Miles and Phoebe held each other close and walked into the night.

About

Green Bike
a group novel

by
Kevin Rabas,
Mike Graves
and Tracy Million Simmons

About Green Bike

Green Bike began as a writing exercise of the Emporia Writers, an independent meeting group of the Kansas Authors Club. The project started as shared files on the group's Facebook page. All members of the group were invited to participate using a McGuffin—the green bike—as the symbol that would unite the stories.

Entries were posted as they were completed, in the same order as they appear in this book. The project started in September, with the final chapters being completed around March of the following year.

"It was a challenge that tested me on many levels," said Tracy Million Simmons. "To write something and immediately share it with multiple readers, without the usual levels of internal processing—read, rewrite, read, rewrite—that my work usually undergoes, was a big step for me as a writer."

Rabas a former jazz musician and continuing jazz and Beat literature aficionado said he felt at home with this novel's improvisatory structure. "Although improvisatory," Rabas said, "the story hangs together. It's a cohesive narrative, not just an exercise. A good deal of thought went into the story's characters, and, although the plot was not predetermined, we knew the strengths and limitations of the characters—what they would do and would not do—and fittingly character drove and determined plot, as did the sensibilities of the three writers. We know each other, and we know what kinds of tales we might be capable of. Beyond that, we pushed ourselves—and our characters. When it felt like something (a scene, an arc in the plot) was going slack, one's coauthors would turn up the heat and test us all."

In early guidelines for the project participants, Mike Graves wrote, "We're using the green bike as a common element, and we're writing individual stories… This is tentatively titled, "Love Stories." I think it's the author's

choice as far as building on the same story/characters, but each author is welcome to do so. I liken this to hitting a baseball. We don't know if the next pitch is going to be a fastball or a slider. Just grab a bat and take a swing."

Kevin Rabas and Graves almost immediately began intertwining stories, borrowing each other's characters and affecting the momentum of each other's stories. Simmons's contribution evolved more independently, and became, in her mind, almost a prequel to the story of her co-authors. "At some point I decided I was writing about the origin of the green bike. Where did this classic Schwinn come from, anyway? I was writing the story of the first rider, perhaps, the woman who loved the bike first."

As for the publishing aspect, Rabas said, "We wrote *Green Bike* on a shared, private Facebook page. So only a group of about 20 could see it—and cheer us on. It was not open to the public. Later, we scraped the text from Facebook and formatted the novel ourselves using Adobe InDesign. However, scraping from Facebook sometimes introduced daunting formatting errors, which we took days or weeks cleaning up. Later, I shopped the novel, and got a hit. A publisher with arms in KC and Arizona wanted it, edited it, and sent a contract, but, in the end, we fell on aesthetic differences, and decided to pull the novel, reedit it, and publish it ourselves, following our own unique vision. So, the novel's been around the block. I think we can all say we're satisfied with it now. Hope you are, too. We love how it turned out."

Rabas called the novel "a wild campus romp." He said, "It's at once a love story, a love triangle, a kunstlerroman (artist's way novel), coming of age tale, wild college days tale, and tale about losing an aging loved one. How can it be all of these things? Because it's a novel of parallel tales. We're not just in one narrative. We're in three."

Kevin Rabas co-directs the creative writing program at Emporia State University and edits *Flint Hills Review*. He has four books: *Bird's Horn*, *Lisa's Flying Electric Piano*, a Kansas Notable Book and Nelson Poetry Book Award winner, *Sonny Kenner's Red Guitar*, and *Spider Face: stories*.

Mike Graves teaches Intensive English and TESOL courses at Emporia State University. His writing has appeared in *Thorny Locust*, *Flint Hills Review*, and elsewhere. He has recently finished a novel about a private detective set in 1937 Wichita. When life conjures its riddles, he turns to back roads and baseball for answers.

Tracy Million Simmons is a freelance writer with more than 500 articles in print. Her work includes everything from feature articles in national and niche publications to ghostwritten material for busy health professionals. She is the yearbook editor for the Kansas Authors Club. Her novel, *Tiger Hunting*, was published in 2013 and was the winner of the 2013 J. Donald Coffin Memorial Book award.

Acknowledgements

Green Bike has been a journey of collaborations and we owe many individuals our thanks for helping us along the way. Thanks, first, to the members of the Emporia Writers Group and the crew at Java Cat Coffeehouse for providing us with drinks and a fine spot to meet on a monthly basis.

We can't say enough kind things about Dave Leiker for our lovely cover and author photos. Take a moment to view Dave's marvelous work at prairiedust.net.

We would also like to take a moment to thank our cover designer, Eric Sonnakolb (www.ericsonnakolb.com) and Jessica Gaddis for early assistance with format and interior design.

Thanks also go to Julie Edmonds for "scraping" the text for this novel from Facebook and to Joyce Rabas for initial copy editing and proofing. Ed Emmer, a fellow Java Cat Coffeehouse frequent flyer, gets credit for the formatting and publishing idea. Thanks to Lulu of Monarch Tattoo (Emporia) for allowing us to shoot photos of her bike and to artist Beth King for the original line drawing of our green bike.

Thanks to *I-70 Review* for allowing us to reprint Mike Graves's poem, "The Ones That Got Away." Also, "Eureka Springs Blues" first appeared in *Thorny Locust*.

Sincerely,
Kevin, Mike & Tracy

WWW.MEADOWLARK-BOOKS.COM

Meadowlark is an independent publisher, born of a desire to produce high-quality books for print and electronic delivery. Our goal is to create a network of support for today's independent author. We provide professional book design services, assuring that the stories we love and believe in are presented in a manner that enhances rather than detracts from an author's work.

For all the debate about the state of publishing today, we remain optimistic. Readers continue to seek quality stories and writers have more opportunities than ever before.

We look forward to developing a collection of books that focus on a Midwest regional appeal, via author and/or topic. We are open to working with authors of fiction, non-fiction, poetry, and mixed media. For more information, please visit us online at www.meadowlark-books.com.

www.ingramcontent.com/pod-product-compliance
Lightning Source LLC
Chambersburg PA
CBHW060226180626
46813CB00007B/2972